The Oldest Bitch Alive

The Oldest Bitch Alive

Morgan Day

LONDON

({i})

({i}) is the standard representation of life. The figure is made of three parts:

    i – the self
    {} – cosmic matter
    () – the physical form

The Orb

On the day Gelsomina contracts worms, she is no different from who she has always been – an animal walking on all fours. The old French bulldog rifles through leather flowers and fruit bushes. She rolls in dry soil, then sniffs the belly of a fallen starling. Her thirst steers her to the murky backyard lake. She laps water with blue-green foam, gulping pollen and minibeasts. It is rich in flavor, an oily muck she likes. Along with sludge, an opaque egg carrying five parasitic worms drifts into her system, beginning their migration from the mouth to the intestines. Gelsomina wanders up a gentle slope to the glass house. Wendy opens the door as she arrives, reaching down with a towel to rub her wet paws. Clean and dry, Gelsomina enters the living space, leaps onto a heather tweed chaise, and falls to sleep within the dunes of a fur throw.

The parasitic worms are lumped together in a pale orb that shed from the swollen band of another worm's mouth. A temperate and moist interior supports their motility. Before Gelsomina consumed them, they felt the vibrations of footsteps on the other side of the orb, the brush of mist off the water. The orb bobbed with the wind, and their bisexual forms tangled, emitting loud pops. Each held private hopes for life beyond the gelatinous habitat: *the world must be bright and open; it will present warm, liquid opportunities.* Like oyster flour, they imagined their next domain to be velvety and acidic, and that they would become shiny and hard.

It was sudden when the orb turned to midnight. The worms assumed they were no longer facing the sun. The structure of time did not affect their sleep, so they waited for the hazy ball to emerge again and stimulate tremors of life. In extended darkness, the worms sent signals to one another about relocation. They huddled together for warmth.

Amid the worms' panic, a figure appears understandable through the shape of its three parts. It is a maze that each being confronts shortly before death. ({i}) hovers above the worms as a remarkably distinct image, discernible despite their lack of eyes. Light receptors trace its outline against the black. Following the appearance of ({i}), the worms hatch. Three are dead upon arrival. The remaining two recoil at the shriveled dead worms and entwine like a ball of thread.

The French bulldog is brindle and compact, with a square head and wrinkles folding around a snub nose. She is on the smaller side of the breed, dwarfed in length but not weight. Gray fur spreads from her flat snout, and tawny streaks have gone blonde. White darts up the chest, while the insides of her erect ears are starkly visible and a gummy pink. She strains to see through a cataract fog. Of the other things to know about Gelsomina: she loves seclusion, her flower is jasmine, and *a gift from God* is her name.

Gelsomina's gut bloats with the worms' intimacy. She struggles to move among the chaise lounge, the side yard where she relieves herself, and two stainless-steel bowls for food and water. Thirst, more than hunger, directs her movements. Not even a hunk of liverwurst is appealing, but she drinks whenever her bowl is filled. The worms stir nausea in Gelsomina and bloody her stools. She is battered by relentless fatigue.

With an innate sense of each worm, Gelsomina deciphers their gestures and feelings. She learns the personalities driving them to engage with her in ways that violate her beliefs of right and wrong. These include the desire to take what is not their own, their comfort with this dynamic, and their saying things about her that she cannot know herself. The longer she shares her form, the more Gelsomina realizes that she has lost an essential organization, one built across years and structured by privacy. The invasion is profound.

The worms make a simple home of Gelsomina. For twenty-four hours, they are in love. Prone to monogamy, their tethered forms convey a term of union: *my pair*. Unlike the young flatworms that live in the gills of fish and permanently fuse during adolescence, Gelsomina's worms are soon tempted by the vastness of her. They unwind in pursuit of a greater place, traversing her internal organs like bucking goats.

But the placidity of the orb did not prepare them for a container of these proportions swinging them in uncharted currents. The journey is not as pleasing as when they awaited rupture into a realm that looked buttered and purred. Life will never be what it once was, when they felt like the only beings to exist. The worms discreetly blame each other.

Gelsomina is partly at fault for the failure of their love. Her body is a disappointment to one of the worms, because it is inhibitive, shaped by a weak immune system and lacking energy. The French bulldog is not the right setting for the worms, who prefer the tissue of cats. The worm's complaints are administered for days, concerning its pair who, after settling in Gelsomina's gastrointestinal tract, is prepared to stay put. There is food to eat and there are places to burrow. Soon, this contented worm thinks, they will proliferate like mad. If only the mucus at their centers could coagulate, if their ends could touch.

Its unhappy pair expected a different life on the other side of the orb: a soft earth plane, scintillating puddles of water. Light would arrive and depart in long arcs, a perpetual summer solstice. The disappointed worm refuses to agree with its pair about the pervasive nature of their situation, that darkness is everywhere. Thoughts of alternative sensations arrive in blurry shades of amber. For a moment, an exit. Briefly, an eclipse. Failing to reconcile, the worms disentangle, wrenching apart when their bare sides brush.

There are many orbs and none are the same. This reality has long affected the meaning and origin of the word *orb*. It is celestial, a plump heavenly body. It refers to a sphere, a monarchy, or a thing in orbit. It is used to describe a body of soldiers positioned in the shape of a circle. An *orbita* is the socket in the skull that holds an eye. Its Latin etymology traces to *orbis*, encompassing many circular objects. The Greek word for *orbit* is linked to *trajectory*, or *course*. This last vestige offers meaning to the worms' situation. They have strayed off course, tumbling into a mock symbiosis, straining to make sense of cohabitation.

Orbs of light appear in photographs and are occasionally seen by the naked eye. These orbs are manifestations of energy, a type not yet understood by people. A true orb must be solid without spokes, emitting light equally in all directions. A blue orb is commonly known as an angel, spirit, or guide. It is a form of communication from a divine figure assuring a being that they are not alone. Some people claim to have seen figures within orbs and therefore believe they are portals. It is common for a being to feel that they have been born into the wrong orb. Others, like Gelsomina, function as a makeshift orb themselves, offering life to those within them.

The acronym ORBS refers to Object Recognition Breakdown Syndrome, or the feeling when one faces an object, experience, or event that is entirely unknown and that no existing ideas can be projected upon. ORBS articulates what, for Gelsomina, had once been unfathomable. With little to do, she focuses on the presence of the worms. She questions whether the name she has for them, their shapes and actions, are her own invention. Alone with her infection, she counts the flicks of the twain creatures like a pulse.

Gelsomina expects the worms to pass through her as other illnesses have come and gone, but this species of parasite persists in the warm-blooded for decades. They occupy cysts in the brain, lungs, and muscle tissue, and are easily transferable. People who live with cats or dogs carrying the parasite regularly receive it themselves, becoming impulsive, aggressive, and violent. They are prone to dangerous activities and suicide; are more likely to die in car accidents due to road rage; take purposeless risks; develop schizophrenia, bipolar disorder, or an anxiety disorder; engage in submissive sexual activity; and become entrepreneurs. A healthy immune system typically protects an infected person from illness. If the person becomes immunocompromised, symptoms can flare, affecting their behavior as well as causing blurred vision, confusion, and a loss of motor skills.

The worms' effects are visible in Gelsomina's slouch and the exaggeration of her head tilt to the right. She does not walk in circles, but her path from one destination to the next is made in consecutive half-loops. Colors are brighter and sounds are louder. The worms are accepted with a hushed, motionless stance and a contemplation of heat. Gelsomina's trunk weighs heavily with their anger. She listens to them describe the worst parts of her, all the problems she did not know she had, such as the quality of the food and shelter she offers and the limitations of her vitals.

This is the first time that she has experienced an unruly thing. In moments of frustration, she wishes she could birth them. It is rare that the worms sing. Most often they fight, and it is always the same argument over and over again, hashed out in the fetal position. They mention leaving, perseverance, and a better attitude. *There is nowhere to go,* they both argue, each in their own defense.

Gelsomina is not sure when or where the worms will go, nor in what way. It is still a mystery to her as to how they appeared, but she is certain they are from the outside. The day was glanced over due to its regularity. The date and time of her infection, and the duration of the worms' inhabitance, are irrelevant. Chronological thinking does not structure Gelsomina's life. It is the site of the infection that asserts meaning. Symptoms arrive sporadically, causing confusion, though she has been disoriented lately for reasons lost on her.

If the worms entered her like food, then they must exit through the same system. She anticipates a difficult bowel movement to relieve herself of them. When she is not constipated, Gelsomina examines her feces in search of the two worms until the man or the woman tells her to stop. To her knowledge, there has been nothing yet that resembles the worms. She envisions them as long and paper thin.

She also questions whether she wants the worms to be alive when they come out. It might be disturbing to discard the dead. She has little experience with the completion of a being besides her encounters with the overturned insects littering the interior borders of the house. The process, as in a being's passage from moving to unmoving, is obscure to Gelsomina. She has never seen it happen, and therefore it must occur on the exterior of the house before making its way in. Considerations of death aside, most of all, she wants her suffering to cease.

Gelsomina closes her eyes, and the worms momentarily interlace. Even tied in a knot, they are resentful of each other. She flips on her back to see if gravity pulls them in a direction they prefer. Nothing appeases them.

The worms make her sick with their hysteria, how they bicker and thrash. To end their arguments, the longer worm says something sharp, and the shorter worm resorts to a pointed silence.

The universe evolved as a round shape like the orb, composed among other bubble universes in a bed of foam. Of the 10^{500} types of bubble universes, each is governed by its own laws. Froth marks the trivial, like the beginning of life when everything could have so easily popped. Instead, light filters through. Foam regenerates across scales. It seethes in mouths and where oceans meet land, is natural and synthetic, vanishes instantaneously, and biodegrades across hundreds of years. Upon completion, the fleeting explosions hiss and fizz.

Both the largest and smallest entities are constructions of foam. In a vacuum of empty space is an effervescent sea of subatomic particles popping in and out, a potent fluctuation of space and time. Within the aggregate are wormholes, unstable shortcuts from one point to another, described as two mouths connected by a throat. The discontented worm lodged inside Gelsomina is an unknowing disciple of the notion that the smallest entities glean existence from the largest, rather than the other way around, as it once again seeks the whole.

The screeching and lightweight material, too, is a world-building substance utilized in architectural models, and worked into structures as insulation, décor, trim, and soundproofing. Mealworms and superworms digest polystyrene foam, reducing waste, although the creatures do not enjoy eating the substance. Many worms despise synthetic foaming agents and will flee from treated soil to a decontaminated site.

The shorter, melancholy worm returns to ({i}) as a way out of Gelsomina. It tries to explain the figure to its pair but has no ability for comparison. Sensations are not easily translated into shapes. Its pair is reluctant to admit that it, too, observed ({i}) looming over the five of them in shifting intensities of brightness, as though proximity allowed them to have dreamt the same dream. The shorter worm is adamant that the figure has more meaning than a shared hallucination and believes that ({i}) controls the passage of beings to different universes. This worm seeks to arrive at its own solutions, instead of with its pair, and lead a life in submission to ({i}).

Autonomy is not a physical endeavor, as the shorter worm initially understood and requires unlearning. The worm started as five, then two. Now, it wants to be one. It perceives its capabilities to reproduce on its own. The worm is not wrong. There are methods for one to become two. Stuck with an unfavorable mate, the worm can start *selfing* – reproducing on its own. But tipping the balance could spawn inbreeding depression. The few offspring that hatch will struggle to survive.

It has long been debated whether a worm cut in half makes two worms. Some believe that if the cut is good and clean, each half of the worm will regenerate to become full. On the odd occasion, the half worm makes another tail, rather than the head that is needed, resulting in a quick and off-kilter existence. More resilient worms can be cut in thirds, with each piece growing a new brain, mouth, and set of hearts. The three of them will eat and swim within one week. They will all retain the memories and personality of the original worm. In these ways, a worm does not really need another worm – its pair.

The Glass House

i. HOUSE OF WORSHIP

Gelsomina lives with a retired couple in a glass house on a lake. John was once a practicing architect, and Wendy was an interior designer. They share a taste for furniture and space, a minimalism caused by a desire for control in the chaos of an urban environment. They moved from New York City to the glass house fifteen years ago, blaming a flooding transportation system, limited access to nature, noise, and light pollution. Their house is located on the outskirts of a small town in the foothills of the Blue Ridge Mountains with a population of less than two thousand people. It sits like a trinket on a peninsula surrounded by pine trees. This is the only place in the country where land is deeded to God.

Neither John nor Wendy is religious, though they were raised in Catholic households. They discuss the architecture of megachurches, whether a house of worship can operate out of a warehouse, and how parishioners are treated as consumers. They like the locals' hand-drawn billboards, which are small and intimate with the road and ask simple questions like *Have you walked with God today? Have you received Him?* Their conversation turns to what they receive. Perhaps the sensorial, the stimulating luxuries of the everyday, such as a cup of coffee or sitting in sunlight.

They are enlightened while engaging with specific works of art. For Wendy, these are Roni Horn's solid-cast glass sculptures. From afar the pieces look like pastel water wells revealing the inconsistencies of light and shadow in an impure world. They are soft and delicate, though each weighs 5 tons. Wendy finds religion in the possibility for a person to meet an artist through the essence of the objects they make.

For John, spirituality surfaces while engaging with fifteen untitled pieces by Donald Judd in Marfa, Texas. The series of concrete boxes are splayed out on desert land, each 2.5 × 2.5 × 5 meters in size, and 25 centimeters thick. While standing in the shade of the structures, he considered the artist's point that two of the three main aspects of visual art – material, space, and color – remain invisible to observers. Judd's belief that space and color are overlooked confirms for John that there is much left for him to discover. The couple's analysis ends with the point that the pastor is essentially a performance artist, that both churches and museums take money, and that they are consumers of art.

People travel from around the country to visit the lake but rarely make it into town. On Main Street, the desecrated brick face of an abandoned hotel draws a few tourists who stand in its center taking pictures of plants climbing through blasted-out windows. Visitors are more likely to go to the nearby Healing Springs, a modest collection of dirty water that rises two inches and pools around a spigot. They collect the water in milk jugs, lugging it home for themselves and their diseased relatives. When the Springs are empty, an employee from the Regional Conservation District tests the water for radiological contamination, ensuring that the Springs remain *relevant, excellent, and visible*. Two regulars at the Springs collect the water for their coffee because it will not leave lime in the pot.

The history of the lake was told to Wendy and John by the realtor when they purchased the glass house. In the center of hundreds of thousands of acres of land bought by a power company, they built a manmade lake to cool the reactors at a nuclear station and generate hydroelectric power. To do so, they dammed four rivers. It took two years to fill and created 18,000 acres of shoreline. Now, warm water is funneled from the nuclear power plant at high speed back into the lake. Deep beneath the surface is a lost city where buildings remain intact, though many are flipped on their sides. This gives the lake a haunted feeling for Wendy and John. While floating together off their dock, they imagine New York City beneath them. Manhattan Island fits neatly into the shape of the cove. They point out the rough location of their last apartment, near a sandbar dominated by a gaggle of geese.

Forested land is delineated by a stone gate. The neighborhood is a curved stretch of one hundred homes running a length of shoreline. For most, these are second homes. On the weekends, owners and guests take out speedboats, towing young people on boards and children desperately gripping inflatable tubes. They meet each other for dinner at a clubhouse overlooking the final hole of a golf course. During early hours, fishers cut the glassy surface in boats so low the men look like they are submerged.

ii. HOUSE OF CARDS

The house was constructed of three primary materials: a glass facade, polished concrete flooring, and wood-paneled ceilings. It was designed by William Brown, an architect who owns a practice of the same name responsible for the appearance of many homes along the lake. His office is sandwiched between a hairdresser and a women's clothing store, with four desks for himself, his receptionist, and two designers who are not yet licensed to practice. William boasts his commitment to style – all those available to him – which he argues is *sans ego* and involves taking existing aesthetic choices and working with his clients to make them their own. His design approach is not site specific, but people, taste, and belief specific.

With this project, William borrowed elements from the Glass House by Philip Johnson, built in 1949 in New Canaan, Connecticut, which was inspired by Mies van der Rohe's Farnsworth House, built between 1945 and 1951 in Plano, Illinois. The 1,500-square-foot historic Farnsworth House is a glass rectangle with all the living on display. It was designed as a weekend retreat and remembered as one of the most important works of the Modernist movement. The Glass House by Johnson is similar, encompassing 1,815 square feet, with one centrally located glass door leading outside. Both were realized as spaces for viewing the surrounding landscape. Neither has interior walls, though there are rooms. Philip Johnson said the Glass House is the only place where, while seated in a swivel chair, you can watch the sun set and the moon rise at the same time.

William Brown swiveled in his desk chair as he researched both designs. He envisioned the experience of two celestial bodies rising synchronously on either side of him. In this position, one must feel at the center of everything. He liked that Johnson's layout could easily be that of a colonial home. William's plans for the house arose smoothly until he came across an interview with Johnson. A quote from the architect tore apart his fantasy of creating a replica of the two glass house originals, only much larger, and therefore, in his opinion, more impressive: 'The Glass House artistically, of course, is a descendant of Mies van der Rohe. He said you could do a glass house one day in the forties and I said you couldn't because a glass house means that if you have a wall that sticks into the glass and then you've destroyed the glassness of the glass house. Therefore, you couldn't have any walls.'

The challenge that William Brown faced in designing a descendent of the glass houses was that his client, the original owners, wanted a 4,000-square-foot home wrapped in glass with many different rooms for their family of four to traverse. Their request required interior barriers and doors, leading the design astray from the open floor plans of its architectural lineage. The result was two stacked Johnson glass houses with a few traditional white walls gingerly snaking across both floors. The house functions as a bridge, straddling a slight dip at the center of the site with a protected pond. At the suspended midpoint of the house, Brown inserted glass flooring, an observation deck in miniature.

The original owners sought a home that was modern, innovative, sustainable, and future thinking. They received a structure that achieved these loose attributes, though not necessarily what one would call a home. It was more so a blank canvas, or the set of a play, where actors might soliloquize by a window. According to onlookers, it was made for a science fiction movie, within which a man would invent a technology to end the world. From their couch, the family waved to their neighbors driving by, signaling that they had been invited in for a drink. One woman commented, in awe, that the house was like a giant crystal as she raised her diamond ring to its facade.

Regardless of the incidents that have taken place within a glass house, it cannot absorb feeling. Emotions are scattershot, ricocheting off walls, ceilings, and impenetrable flooring. Contrary to the glass house, the traditional family home absorbs emotion into its pillows, blankets, carpets, curtains, and many places to rest, eventually reaching a tipping point when too much history has been stuffed in its fabric. Years of loving, sighing, yelling, and hiding burst from the material. Fluffing the pillows might unleash a violent argument from decades past. In this way, a glass house offers an infinite fresh slate.

When Wendy and John moved in, they were surprised by the austerity. The house was like a deck of cards. Vacant, the details holding the structure together showed at its edges. The first object they put in the house was a long-cherished glass vase intended to hold their memories of the city while functioning as an ode to the larger structure. But the vase only amplified the nakedness of their new living situation. Its transparency could never embody their past.

Wendy went along the property line snipping long grasses and cattails, which she arranged in the vase, temporarily positioned on the kitchen island beside a steel espresso machine and a bag of coffee beans from their favorite café. John unloaded the few critical items they brought with them by car before the movers arrived with the bulk of their things. On the floor were tote bags of cleaning supplies, toilet paper, bath towels, blankets, bed linens, and pillows.

John took photos of the lake shyly lapping at red dirt. Without knowing what to do with herself, and in avoidance of the conversation neither of them wished to have about the starkness of the glass house, Wendy cleaned smudges from the windows. She grew tired as she worked from sheath to sheath. Levitating on the glass floor above the pond, she saw her bare footprints replicated on its surface. Looking closely, she also saw John's footprints, as well as those of another person. Her attention to the structure, its upkeep, would have no end.

There are a few additional factors that separate a glass house from one wrapped in wood, brick, adobe, or stucco. A being in a glass house must at some point disappear. Otherwise, they look like they are in the center of a field. They are exposed above a body of water and can be viewed from across its shores by people who understand the house as a pretentious domus. At a distance, the furniture recedes as shadows. The unmoving figures disrupt the flow of beings who take turns sitting on their laps. At night, the beings are on a backlit stage: retrieving and transporting objects, touching the form of another. They can see no one, but everything can see them.

A glass house is a chemical outcome of sand, soda ash, and limestone. Its foundation bears the weight of emptiness. Exposure demands its use, which instructs the actions of those living inside. A glass house is a discussion of fear; it is a lifestyle of uncertainty. Abandoned, the windows quiver. Sound gets trapped in right angles. Though fragile and lucid, if a glass house is demolished, its pieces will decompose across the earth for the next one million years.

It is said that those living in a glass house should not throw stones. *Judge not, that you be not judged.* To decide to live in a glass house is to admit no fault. It is a statement of morality. For the immoral, to disappear is difficult and relies on scrim curtains. It is best to have a windowless room to conduct faults. Or, like Johnson's circular brick restroom, to relieve oneself.

William Brown designed a pavilion on the second floor that functions like an unearthed bunker illuminated in artificial light. It is a place to rest one's head on a desk, to tunnel vision, and to let the guard down. Wendy and John use this room as storage space for architectural models of the single-family residences they designed throughout their careers. When either of them feels lost or uninspired by their routine in the country, they admire the miniatures of their life's work, wiping dust from Styrofoam with a damp rag, and rearranging tiny plastic people.

Over time, the glass house has remained the same. Wendy and John are not prone to rearranging their spaces, preferring to have a few enduring items organized in ways that feel central to the spirit of each piece. The couple's design plans are on a much grander scale, concerning the dominance of one material. Since the day of their arrival, when Wendy realized that her attention to the glass-ness of the structure was interminable, the couple has considered whether to add another material to the facade. The most sensible approach would clad parts of the exterior in stone veneer. They debate whether the design move would compromise the integrity of the structure or simply open a can of worms.

Even though Wendy and John are designers, when reduced to people living in a space, they get caught up in the fact that the facade is also the interior walls. They do not like that someone outside the house can see them both while they might not see each other. There must be an exterior and an interior marked by a protective barrier, one that does not allow a person to get lost in between.

iii. HOUSE-TRAINED

Wendy and John do not have children. They always wanted a French bulldog, a breed with personality and what they call *a miraculous display of expression.* Their life in New York City – spending the day at a museum, attending a show, going out for late dinners – did not allow for a dog. A rural setting necessitated a domesticated animal. When they placed their new puppy on the living room rug, her presence surprised them. They could not put their finger on why, but it had something to do with the sharp contours of the glass house and Gelsomina's stout, compact figure. It amused them to see her in the foreground of a fertile landscape and placid lake, like a painting that was meant to frame a lounging woman but instead featured a French bulldog.

Gelsomina did not like the house in her younger years, much less the earth, water, machinery, and beings on the other side of the glass. The house clicked and groaned, turning off and on. Her days were populated by the theatrics of television, the announcements of microwaved food and fully heated ovens, the glow of laptops, and the strange faces and voices emitted from many different apps. She was encouraged to watch blurry minute-long clips accompanied by the sound of a barking dog.

She liked the flesh of the man and the woman, their scents and high-pitched voices. Gelsomina moved in their shadows. When they were absent, the dark shapes they produced were lifted and she moved freely. It was an independence she did not ask for. Half a foot off the ground, she scratched wood doors and smeared her wet snout across the glass, wishing to burst through. She defecated across hard and soft textures, and dug into blankets, sofas, and chairs. The agony of their absence ripped a straight line up her abdomen and into her throat. Gelsomina held the eruption of emotion in her mouth, which dissipated in neat quivers down her back.

As their car pulled into the long driveway, she rushed to the front door and shot upward on her back legs. She licked their fingertips and bit their toes as they removed them from their shoes. She ran to the living room to grab a plush toy and returned to shake it violently at their feet. Her love for them was almost too much to bear. Most dishonorable were the trips they took as a couple, leaving her behind to persist through daily visits from a stranger, and from whom Gelsomina hid as he filled food and water bowls. He sat on a barstool, wiping sweaty palms over the countertop, and twisting to look out over the water. If he glanced in her direction, Gelsomina growled.

When the couple returned to her, she returned to herself. She felt kindred to the woman on some days, the man on others. Gelsomina curled like the woman into the large sectional couch and was attentive to headlights flashing across the windows. She studied loud noises, remaining stock-still. When she ate, it was controlled, and when the woman told her to *go potty*, she padded lightly across the stone path. With the man, Gelsomina followed his confident steps. She finished meals with pride, her nub of a tail straight out like a blunted arrow. She partook in the removal of dead leaves and followed at his heel to retrieve garbage cans from the curb. His frustrations enthralled Gelsomina as she barked alongside him.

She could smell the passage of time, and therefore the patterns that gave shape to their days. Weak odors revealed old habits, while strong odors were of the present. She knew the sex of the man and the woman, their health, moods, and stresses. Together, the couple was happiest about food and drink. They were most relaxed first thing in the morning and again in the evening. With both, she stood on their laps to look deeply into their eyes. It hurt her to detect even a flicker of sadness. Their concerns were her concerns, though she could not decipher the root of their problems. Gelsomina's response involved lying longways on their legs and repeatedly licking the top of a hand as an expression of empathy in the only way she knew how.

No matter how Gelsomina morphed herself, the man and the woman were bound to each other, and she was left out of a lopsided love among the three of them. They communicated softly, retreating behind closed doors. In these moments, there were a few behaviors she could name for certain. The nature of their footsteps, for one. Some atmospheres, too. There were six emotions detected and studied: anger, fear, happiness, sadness, surprise, and disgust. All to say that prior to the worms, she had never considered her own.

iv. HOUSE RULES

Gelsomina envisions the couple's movements in their first-floor bedroom based on their sounds, and because Wendy once broke the rule of where she is allowed. It was many years ago when Gelsomina was a puppy. The man had left for a few days. An orange glow rested over the house, and Wendy carried Gelsomina for the first time through the threshold of the primary bedroom and into the bathroom, where she placed her on a white bathmat. Gelsomina watched as she turned a knob and water gushed into the tub. Wendy stripped her clothes and lowered with Gelsomina into the warm water.

Her first instinct was to get out. To prevent her from scratching slick edges, Wendy held Gelsomina tightly against her chest, until she grew comfortable with the water encompassing their bodies. With Gelsomina tentatively perched on her belly, Wendy poured a line of liquid soap down her back. She scrubbed her in circles with the floral scent. Rinsed and fragrant, Gelsomina was placed back on the bathmat and rubbed with a plush towel. Wendy clasped her collar, to which she had tied a pink bow. It was the beginning of Gelsomina's lifelong fascination with their bathroom.

From then on, whenever the couple accidentally left their bedroom door open, Gelsomina slunk in and relieved herself on the white bathmat. There was no way to explain herself, no meaning or motive behind the act. It had become so routine that most of the time she realized only after the fact that she had defecated. Their bath together seemed to have relevance that returns to Wendy in recent months. Gelsomina does not understand the gesture, but lately Wendy ties a rainbow of different bows to her collar. Rather than bathe her, she takes lavender-scented wipes and runs them twice daily down Gelsomina's back, up her stomach, and across the pads of her paws. She cleans between her wrinkles and applies petroleum jelly to her dry snout.

v. HOUSE OF NOTHING

The neutral palette of the glass house creates a cold and direct experience that Gelsomina has grown to identify with over time. In her old age, she is reserved, at times stoic, and keeps to herself. Tenderness is delivered subtly, requiring the recipient to be attuned to her mannerisms, like a being who can hear sounds at lower frequencies than most. Gelsomina does not mind the minimal furniture but in her infected state wishes that there were more places to hide, particularly when sunlight pierces though the glass.

Most of her days are spent on a small bed positioned in front of the fireplace. Regardless of the season, the fireplace is lit. It floats on the first floor in between the dining room and living room as a balance beam. The orientation loosely mimics Philip Johnson's approach: 'The living room is a raft that floats in its proper position vis-à-vis the fireplace. The rug is the living room. The living room also sits on its lawn in the same way that the rug sits on the Glass House.'

Sometimes an animal stops in the yard to take a long look at Gelsomina. She returns their stares, no longer possessing the energy to chase them from the property. She is used to conducting sterile interactions across a transparent barrier. This has changed with the arrival of the worms. Gelsomina wants to remove herself from view, an evolution of a response to shame that she has had since she was young. After chewing on a leg of furniture, or attempting to run upstairs, and facing the disappointment of the couple, she lodged herself beneath a wooden television console, about five feet long and two and a half feet tall. Now, she seeks to conceal the changes that might reveal her contagion.

Gelsomina shuffles under the wooden console and rests along the cool length of the wall. Sound is muffled and vibrates: the murmur of the television, the hiss of the espresso machine, the varied thuds of the couple's bare footsteps. Under there, she can think clearly about the glass house for what it is: a behemoth that will never be impartial, a thing that will always be *consisting of.* For example, *consisting of* her in its reflections, *consisting of* her bodily fluids across the floor. She wonders about her role as a parasite in the chambers of the home, and if she is like a worm. The thought is comforting, aligning Gelsomina with the sleek glass house as they confront the other lives within them.

Gelsomina rolls over, and she is momentarily interrupted by a string of cobwebs attached to the tip of her nose. Her mind drifts to the idea that she is simultaneously shrinking and expanding – the limbs, the gut. She compares herself to what she can. She fits beneath the console as about one fifteenth of its size. She can fit in a drawer, but she cannot fit in the palm of a hand. The worms, who are recklessly moving across her lower half, can fit in the palm of a hand, also the pit of a stomach, the ring of a mouth, and an anus.

They have not reached one month of age, yet the worms surpass her in having a more complete picture of the interconnection of all beings. Gelsomina criticizes her confinement, and the distractions inside the house, for her lack of knowledge. For instance, in the corner of the living area is an obtuse woven basket that gets emptied of dog toys throughout the day, then filled up again by Wendy and John before they go to sleep. The toys are predominantly solid in color, shapes rather than characters, besides the few animated outliers gifted by friends and family.

There is one toy that does not fit beneath the wooden console, a cream plush ball that is almost too large for Gelsomina to carry. The object is one of her preoccupations. She carries it everywhere, even though it blocks her vision, and she regularly tumbles over the front of it. The plush ball receives all her emotions, expressed through the placement of her teeth, how she kneads it and folds it beneath her. Unlike her other toys, Gelsomina has not yet ripped open the plush ball to remove the squeaker from its center. The once soft material of the toy is now crusted and damp from her sucking on it. The repetitive act, *nooking*, releases endorphins, soothing her anxiety.

Before consuming the worms, her primary concern was that she was a burden. Gelsomina occupies a similar role as the glass house in her old age – a thing that requires maintenance. Or perhaps she is closer to a piece of weathered furniture, one that is not used but passed down for sentimental reasons. She knows that her body is a hindrance. Arthritis has caused her hips to gradually curl further beneath her, so that she struggles to jump onto the couch and chaise lounge. Her vision is clouded by circles of light. Sleep waffles in and out, leaving Gelsomina to spend midnight hours licking open a scab between the pads of her front left foot. The habit worsens with her allergies in the early spring and fall and is aggravated by stepping in real grass. The side yard, where she relieves herself, is too far for her now. By the time her bladder feels full, or there is pressure in her rectum, Gelsomina cannot practice restraint.

At first, she thought it would be easier for the couple if she relieved herself in the same spot, where they rarely stand, on the concrete floor beneath a painting that they do not stop to admire. The piece has a yellow-green background splattered with black that pools in the center, like balsamic vinegar in olive oil. Once she made regular use of the space beneath the painting, the couple discouraged her from going there, picking her up as she teetered over. Gelsomina also gags up small puddles of bile, likely from the volume of grass she consumes to quell her nausea.

Wendy is no longer fazed by Gelsomina's relief spread across the house. She covers the couch in blankets and has rolled up their more expensive rugs. She maintains a process for cleaning the dirtied blankets and applying new ones from an adjacent linen closet, which begins with her closing Gelsomina in the laundry room and putting on gloves. She carries the soiled blankets to the washer, tosses the gloves, washes her hands, then applies new blankets, tucking the edges between the cushions of the couch. Gelsomina is released and returns to the living area, where she relishes the freshly washed linens and falls asleep.

Recently, the couple has prevented Gelsomina from stepping on the vents – steel grates cut into the floor – which blow hot and cold air and, according to Gelsomina, lead to nothing. It is a recent concern of theirs that is more so spurred by Gelsomina's new fascination, rather than anything she has done. They track her path around the vents on the first floor, nudging her away, but Gelsomina does not have plans to pollute the vents. Gazing through the slits, she is drawn by the endlessness of nothing.

vi. HOUSE HOG

Other than the difficulty in moving with her potbelly, Gelsomina is most troubled by the ammonic smell of the worms within her. She maneuvers her putrid form away from the couple as well as another, significantly younger French bulldog they brought home last year – Zampanò. It was strange for the couple to have an exuberant puppy after so many years of leisure with Gelsomina. They had forgotten the maintenance required. Zampanò was taken out every two hours. They rapped their fists on his crate – a space he rapidly outgrew – when he cried in the night.

Taller and more robust, Zampanò falls, rolls over, and sits on Gelsomina as if to suffocate her, though he does not mean to. Zampanò's face is wide and heavily wrinkled. Food dries and hardens on the tip of his flat nose. His jowls are pink and filthy against his black brindle fur. In everything he does, Zampanò huffs as though he is out of breath, even while sleeping. Zampanò appears unhealthy and slow, but he is quick to react to strange noises. When he is not agitated, he can be found searching for scraps of food or seated eagerly beneath the man or the woman as they eat. Unsatiated, Zampanò whimpers.

He is also greedy with affection and inserts himself between the couple and Gelsomina. At first, Gelsomina was disturbed by his aggression. Then, she was frustrated that she was unable to sink into the warm spots of the man and the woman, resting in their tightest corners. Zampanò bothers her less these days. Despite his flaws, they are companions. Gelsomina does not mind the friendship after so many years alone. He offers her a form of unanimity. Their being has an exact likeness; a reflected physicality that separates Gelsomina from the couple.

The two French bulldogs, though stunted, are not innocent. They are not small children without the ability to speak. Rather, they have been forced into an obscure maturation by four walls and their infantilization. They are most of all a product of routine and mundanity. There are no migrations nor hibernations. They have never practiced methods of giving. Sex is opaque. Rain is a hindrance to bowel movements. Food is regular and monochromatic. The two have never prayed nor killed. They roam the backyard at a short distance from each other. Zampanò rushes ahead of Gelsomina, stopping and returning to her before hurrying onward again as if encouraging her to keep up. When he is tired in the evenings, Gelsomina licks the grime from the wrinkles of his face.

Lately, he smells illness on her, but having never experienced it himself, Zampanò does not grasp her debilitation. Gelsomina removes herself from their daily outings, instead conserving her energy to rid herself of the worms. More than once, Zampanò sniffs her back and underside in confusion, and Gelsomina nips at him. He is too juvenile to understand the situation she has found herself in.

vii. HOUSE OF MIRRORS

At the back of the house lies a gradient from stone to artificial turf to a copper shoreline of shallow water, cleared by daylight and extending outward into the dark blue depths of the lake. Long before Gelsomina's encounter with the worms, the land outside the glass house was unpredictable and treacherous. It was where Gelsomina first registered that there is much she will never wholly comprehend, including an obscure source of energy, the Invisible Force.

The Invisible Force mirrors an array of other natural phenomena. It is like an earth shock, which is an earthquake in a localized area following a traumatic incident such as a heavy explosion. There are animals who produce a similar effect, like the snapping shrimp, which opens and closes its claws so rapidly that the surrounding bubbles release energy that shock its prey. A person can go into a state of shock following a sudden drop in blood flow. Once, a woman with tapeworm larvae in her spine reported that the worms released electric shocks down her legs, causing her to fall and stealing away her ability to ride her Friesian horse.

There is a seemingly randomized demarcation of land that cannot be seen, only felt. If Gelsomina and Zampanò accidentally stray outside of this ambiguous area, the Invisible Force zaps them. It has no smell nor pattern, no timing nor warning. They have memorized landmarks to avoid the wrath of the Invisible Force, gathering the scent of bushes and trees that intersect its inconspicuous lines. They agree that the pain is worse than ingesting a bee, a mistake both dogs have made at least twice. The origin of the Invisible Force is unknown and simply another reminder of the cruelty of existence. Coming across the open carcass of an animal confirms for the French bulldogs that it lingered for too long in the path of the Invisible Force rather than moving forward or backward as they have learned to do.

Now that she is forgetting things, Gelsomina regularly wanders into the Invisible Force. Sometimes Wendy or John witnesses her leap into the air for this reason and is racked with guilt. What most bothers Gelsomina is that she has been tricked once again, and that one shock means two. On the other side of the Invisible Force, scouring rushes reach above her head and soil turns to sop. Fearful and sinking, Gelsomina forces her way through the stinging line of electricity to safely return to the property.

Gelsomina is pinned between two notions: the simplicity of an existence that has been long curated for her, and an intimacy with the worms and the outside world. There is much that the dogs will never experience because of the Invisible Force. The mystery of far-off lands, marked by the secretions of other animals, now stirs more curiosity in Gelsomina due to those veritable usurpers. Virgin to experience, the worms are her first scratch at life.

Anatomy of an Apple

I have no more formal boundary, ritual of superficial meaning. Twain creatures heave through me. Nocturnal kickers. Two thieves and a deluge. The throb of the worms in my lower abdomen. My teeth grinding amid giantdoms of glass walls. Could I ever return to how I once was? Before I became a container for miniatures? I thought I was a small being. Surrounding objects with their unreachable heights. Outside the boundless liquid warned as the source itself. Dyad of ecclesiastical agents. How they make themselves at home, hammering out the design of my sustained expansion. There are new concerns. Belching, and where is the origin of that itch? Pain as undergirded heat. A minuscule script of my path in blood across this cool floor; loop of stasis. The days have become nights, too, in that I am conscious throughout of a not-really-sleep. Delirium in figments of fragments gone. A light and airy version of me wades in familiar places, in this house eschewed. And when I wake into a flash of lucidity, I am the same only heavier. The reality of consumption is in my engorged middle. The tingle of another and one other, too. A breeding ground in my squatness. Its members circling the empty pelvic diaphragm. Aerated reminder of my celibacy. At times volitional, but mostly the restraint of material superiority. Maybe I have been hibernating. Maybe I have only lived one long blacked-out season, untutored in fundamental nature. Still, life has begun with all its dismal practices as I gestate clandestine forms. Soma no longer. In uttermost shock the vital strings fiddle me. Cuckold to their strained devotion. Unwilling abbess, head of fail state. Coup of the primordial. I am presently experiencing a perpetual metabolic depression. Where did all the energy go? Exhaustion is one reminder of revolutions of darkness passed. The result of my static place where change happens in the margins. Here I am gleaning how to be from derivatives. And I have always lived beneath where everything appears to take place. A shrunken existence marked by interactions with limited matter. Voices and rattling metal cross higher planes. Suspended hands reaching. Feet slapping against the hard. Until now life had been much more accommodating. I guess I am a colossus figure. And I did not know that the container suffers more than the contained. Every movement of the twain creatures is my injury. A surprise, no less. I look around to see if I am the only one in my precarious position. I have always been aware of the things in this room. My only room. Eternal space. Four corners of an echo chamber. The flat intersections spelled out by sharp light. There must have been a malfunction early in the making of these objects. Their origin leading to their going nowhere. I see how they sit. Feeble pegs upon which they rest. The way, like trees, they hover. In certain light – yellow, gray, soft – their dormancy emits a palpable sadness, the taste of plastic. I have had my own effects on them: the divot where my form has lain, a rotten piece of sinking pasture; marks where younger teeth have gnawed; concentrations of urine in acid whiffs; and the fecal remnants of my past fervor. The mundane constants bend to our whims. In my state, I am reconsidering the emotions of the static objects, closest to me in our daily fodder, and whether they are also homes for twain creatures. Their immobility prevents their itching of interior spots where they might be touched like me. No eyes, face, nor expression. They are quiet unless pushed. Then, screeching at the ankles. Unshed specimens beneath dimpled flanks. Every day they hold their breath. In the corner, a chair is shaped like a shell to hold a man. A fossil in an archaeological site, the innards ripped out and upholstered in the oiled skin of some dead creature. Oh, my frail attempt to find a commiserate partner. I have dealt with them, the objects. I narrowly exist in a space with sixteen large ones. From the man and woman, I have learned their names: couch, coffee table, dining table, six dining chairs, two lounge chairs, three stools, the wooden console, and a rug. Many are only structures to me. Blockish uncanny things. With others, our coexistence is made futile by the man and the woman. Most I am not allowed to touch. They repeat that operative, lonely word: *No*. Since birth, hearing this ignites a fire inside me. If they said what they meant – *stop* – perhaps I would not rampage on in my intimacy with the objects, biting, licking, gnawing, rubbing, and digging. I observe them instead from my penalized stance. Taunting me in their unknowing. The altogether glass structure we reside within looms larger than we know. Viscera of this dwelling. Seeing the couple's idolization of the objects, I am the nonexquisite. A crude entity receiving pats here and there. Other items – steel vents anchored into the floor, sheaths of glass, the buoyant dust, the putty that bulges at the edges of the room and in spots retains a musky scent – arrive and recede as minor backdrops.

When these details drift into the foreground, my attention goes to their recession, much like me as years compile. A thing that bristles in a corner when seen. Beside me, spores consume adhesive connecting floor to glass to ceiling, turning linear boundaries black. Weep holes release inside rain. It is those that make themselves known and available that participate in my study of containment, an analysis of harboring. I am not so strict. Any fine particle will do, so long as it disrupts order. I prefer the ones in the bellies of beasts. For instance, a rock lodged in the foam of the couch. Flaking, golden powder of insides miming flowers and faces and flowers and faces. I analyze the sixteen large objects and try out our differences. I stand atop some – the couch, the lounge chair – make tight circles and rub my form along them. I smell for a chemical signaling discomfort. In the process of turning around, I notice one origin of my recent irritation on the other side of my form. Turned in half there is the mirror of my mouth and gummy throat. A cavity visible, delicate opening that is the excess of my inside. Below are sacs and metallic breath, the rotten smell of fish. Ovals expanding into pink. Cleaning the rim, I have an urge to drag across tightly twisted yarn, the only friction in this glass container. Back there I smell the woman's scent as she once was, occasionally, like meat dropped between her legs. My face pressed into the slink of her. Hands arrive beneath my neck, pushing me out of my position of rubbing. A bubble erupts in my mouth the taste of the steel bowl, the paste of it on my palate. In a fit I smear myself again across the rug, the last of the counted objects, who cannot be analyzed at this time but instead is made responsible for relieving my ailment. Here is the woman's wrist: rose, jasmine, and citrus. Here are her hands to tell me that my engagement with the rug is wrong. A code I have resigned myself to never understand, one that does not show itself when I am alone with the objects. The woman seems to know. The man, too, who carries me by my middle. He picks me up at will and transports my form. As though I maim the objects beyond the sunken pasture of my lethargy. The woman lifts my hips from the rug, rubbing my head with her palm. Concern wades in her eyes. Signal of my growing ill condition. Behind the woman, Zampanò, dribbling house hog and mirror of me, lunges into a four-beat gait. Not like my slow knuckling limbs. Young brute. I am a knockable being, tossable, useful only when believed to be. Does he know of the twain creatures in me? Dumb brute. The root of his ignorance lies in his human neurosis – endless infatuation with the man and woman. Tantrum of ownership. Here he is barging into my two half-selves, as I've rolled myself to make a circle, to become one impenetrable form with no beginning and no end. Flattened, I'm no longer whole. A linear congruence with the rug, if only to blend in. I sniff my spot of attempted relief. As I tremble, the woman is there to push him from me, freeing my form for her examination. Lifting my fifth limb, she looks at my second mouth. Connecting point, a tie-in of proportions. Searching for the reason for my restless behavior. It is right there beaming. Little ridged orbit of mine. Passage of the pliable. A flash of disgust in her upturned lip. The shaking subsides and my thoughts float. Is this my new, forever way? Every inconvenience carries the potential for unending. A toothache, itching. Now, unknown beings. The house hog sniffs my genitals parted in open air. Mostly there is fear in me. But also, the twain creatures, resilient in their crossing of arbitrary borders of my own making. Of my absent mother's own making. No one mentioned they could be trampled over. Disregarded, though coddled onto my back, my head is lolling. Side-to-side, my front limbs suspend. The bottom of the house becomes the top. I have been fixed by the woman more than once before. Today she rises from my splayed form, yet my discomfort persists. How long will I lie here? On the only note of comfort, a woolen landscape? The woman has no pill for me to consume, no scented wipe or rotten spray to fertilize the wounds between my pads. If I were to cry out it would induce domestic panic. We are all engaged in a synthetic knowing. All these acts have played out before. The woman sits on the couch, once again claiming to understand the object better than me. We surrender to the obfuscation of neon light rendered across strange faces of the big screen. The silence of their moving mouths my muted making. I recognize in their expressions the consistent emotion – concern. To the left, a foggy perception. There is me in the glass. Drooping face and black holes for eyes. Consciousness of me. I consider in my precarious position whether I have ever been encountered, that is, prior to the twain creatures. Or, if I have always been a wall. Like this one my other me is caught within. Am I the only one who sees this other me? I must be breaking down, my illegitimate form fading with age. How I wish to sink and forget my transformation. Instead, I watch a green apple from beneath the glass table, flipped in my vision so that it levitates as a crown over a bulbous rump. It rests lonely. A plucked flower, the apple has the fragrance of the earth and therefore does not belong in here. I had been given a slice of one once to eat. Its capable seeds were still vibrating with potential. Sour essence rushing up my tongue. Removed from a life source and on the way to death, yet carrying about like a rooted plant. Essentially, a bogus living like mine. Where does this question come from: is it alive? The apple quivers due to its proximity to me, the house hog, the woman, due to our steps and gestures disturbing the glass. It is not living nor dead, just as I am neither fully living nor fully dead. To reap shame by thinking of the apple as a living object, to ask if the apple is living. It cannot become the tree. Only seeds evolve. To think the same of myself. Where is my tree then? What is my tree? At first, I think it must have to do with a person. Longtime facilitators of my days. Assumptions of beings are banal. My tree is material and structural. I have left behind the shape we are made to hold on to; how we are positioned to others. A false sense of enclosure. If I am the apple, are the twain creatures the seeds? Primed to germinate with wintry moisture and sprout in the aftermath of my decline? And if I continue becoming that which I encounter – I will not be the items in this house. Immovable objects unable to *do*, unto which the *doing* is *done*. Worthless stratification of the proliferate and non. There is much that I now consider containable by me, and therefore I am frightened of, such as insects, a bottle cap, a coin. The man, the woman. I am willing to be the sounds but not the air. Perhaps by embodying noise I will no longer be startled by it. I cannot say how I was shaken from the tree, only that my form refuses to be a tree *part*. The twain creatures refuse it, creating a twain refusal. Seeds unwilling to sprout. Analyzing the shining skin of the apple, it does not look like me. Smooth, self-protected. Perhaps my problem with the apple is that it has no rage. Neutral, waxed form. The problem is that I may become everything in this house.

{ (})

In a study of monkeys and human adults and children published in 2020, a group of researchers reported that the ability to produce recursive sequences may not actually be unique to our species after all. Both humans and monkeys were shown a display with two pairs of bracket symbols that appeared in a random order. The subjects were trained to touch them in the order of a 'center-embedded' recursive sequence such as { ( ) } or ({ }). After giving the right answer, humans received verbal feedback, and monkeys were given a small amount of food or juice as a reward. Afterward the researchers presented their subjects with a completely new set of brackets and observed how often they arranged them in a recursive manner. Two of the three monkeys in the experiment generated recursive sequences more often than nonrecursive sequences such as { (}), although they needed an additional training session to do so. One of the animals generated recursive sequences in around half of the trials. Three- to four-year-old children, by comparison, formed recursive sequences in approximately 40 percent of the trials.

This paper prompted Liao [Diana Liao, a postdoctoral researcher in the lab of Andreas Nieder, a professor of animal physiology at the University of Tübingen] and her colleagues to investigate whether crows, with their renowned cognitive skills, might possess the capacity for recursion as well. Adapting the protocol used in the

2020 paper, the team trained two crows to peck pairs of brackets in a center-embedded recursive sequence. The researchers then tested the birds' ability to spontaneously generate such recursive sequences on a new set of symbols. The crows also performed on par with children. The birds produced the recursive sequences in around 40 percent of trials – but without the extra training that the monkeys required.

> 'Crows Perform Yet Another Skill Once Thought Distinctively Human'. *Scientific American*, November 2, 2022

~

Water cupped us, warm and buoyant. A reliable arc of light rose and fell above a fluid plane. Our forms sank into one another. Sensations were new; our touching and gliding in mist. All five of us tied in a knot were pleased to float on a throbbing surface. Gradually, we popped in unison and left sleep behind. But in an instant, we strayed from the shapelessness to constricted walls and edges. We shook in darkness, sensitive to breath and the gurgling of nether regions in this new universe. Still, we held hope for a return to a pulpy and illuminated terrain.

I trust our conception but cannot accept our emergence. Everything changed when our orb arrived here. And after we hatched, nothing was sacred. All delineations were wiped clean. I curled atop the ruptured orb. In grief, I rapped my ends on its swiftly dissolving pieces. Three were dead at the outset. Bewildered by the pitch-dark, my pair and I enfolded for an unknown length of time, believing that we, too, would die. The fortitude of my blossoming form was gone, replaced by a chattering habit of uncertainty. Yet an enlightened figure carried me, revealing our passage back to what had been there, the orb, and what had been promised, an enraptured state of ({i}).

As novelty faded, we unraveled as individuals. For the first time, I experienced life on my own. I gleaned from textures and tastes an early sense of our surroundings: bitter mucus, intricate folds, an elusive acidity that both pained and pleasured me. In the process, I learned about the significance of crossing into darkness. As a pair we are invisible. I am nothing but a membrane. My pair is nothing but a membrane. I am not certain of my outline. Where do I begin and where do I end? The orb was an extension of me. Then, the partial death of me. Is this organism now an extension of me? Are we all one?

I told this to my pair, and it scoffed. In response to my questions, my pair said that we are trapped in the form of an organism; we are not the organism, just as we are not each other; and we are facing thick walls with no clear exit. My pair thinks I am helped by concrete statements, but I am wounded by the absolute.

My pair does not believe in greater understandings of life, as though thoughts are not reality. I must regard the ideology of my pair because there is no autonomy. There has been little internal guidance to offset the dominance of our matrimony. Our disagreements transform our tubes into bile, an acerbic vertigo that disrupts my interactions with all forms of organic life. I wonder about the other worms, who they were and could have been, who I would be if they had lived. Or, who I would be if I had been released alone with my honest nature divulged. No more drills of practicality nor daydreams stunted by rash calls from my pair to *make do*.

Violent waves of longing persist. In our exchange, I gather that my pair thinks I am a simple creature ruled by elementary feelings. *Truth*, repeats my pair, *is only that which can be experienced.* We have already argued the meaning of truth – an emotion versus a reality – as though it will determine whether we stay in this place. I long to be outstretched, ebullient with discovery, to have my form warmed by abiding light and smell salt through every pore. Are these sensorial hallucinations a lesser truth than this purgatory?

I am shaped by primeval mores. In the orb, we inherited the memories of all the worms who came before us dating back to the first brain. The mass recollection has been retained throughout the evolution of our forms across time; the bubbling of an orb to the fissure of our slinking length; bubble to slink, bubble to slink. As we shed from the interior walls of the orb, this information was imparted to us and used in the construction of our individual beings. With the presence of the past, I have never been disorganized. My path is clear: ({i}). I have the knowledge to be and reproduce on my own. At any point, I can leave and enact a habit of self. Then I remind myself: this is *my pair*!

Neither of us believes in fate, but this might shield our desires for separate futures. We agree that there must be a reason for our living. For me, there must be a reason for our living alongside each other, with all our affection and disagreements. I seek the purpose for our survival over that of the other worms. It cannot just be the making of additional orbs, as my pair says. I believe it must be to do with ({i}). Did ({i}) originate with the first brain? *Is* ({i}) the first brain? Have we returned to a very beginning?

*

Guided by a different objective, my pair has no problem with our inability to leave. My pair prefers to limit the questions of our existence, proceed with our basic functions, and reproduce. As though there were no other place for us to survive, as though there were not more of life for us to find. Perhaps this is due to the very first act required of my pair in this place, one that stunned it into an existence that is steady and known.

After we hatched, I caught my pair discarding the dead. Moving across a silken path, I felt the flesh of my pair, and beside my pair, I felt the static flesh of the three worms. The superstitious response of my pair revealed more to me than I let on. I joined my pair beside the dead. In a soundless huddle we shuttled the shrunken forms to a far edge of the tubular space. There we tried to arrange the dead worms as they were woven in our orb, but their forms had already hardened into the position of rigor mortis. We laid them beside each other with at least one end touching another, making a flat orb.

Without prompting, we both used our forms to call out to the dead. The surroundings vibrated and the fluid within each of us vibrated, too. Warmth flowed from one end of me to the other and back, a fleeting concentration on how I am attached to my pair. It was an act we both instinctively knew to do in that moment, a clear instruction from generations of memory. While gloriously rapping my top end, I made an internal promise to stay with my pair and together reach the joyous sensations of ({i}). Perhaps there is no fate, but yes, a meaning in our union.

To call attention to our shared gesture, I crowded my pair into a corner until there was no space between us, and with a sequence of rhythmic scrunching communicated my emotions in a tangible echo. My pair shrugged me off, and though I felt that all the attention was on me, I was not noticed. I learned that my perception of my pair is limited, and that I would always need to keep a small part of myself concealed.

My pair is perturbed that we contemplate ourselves, but I think that our forms are the first step to comprehending our place here. We are made of the same materials that form our surroundings. With a bit of pressure on my pair, we share our thoughts on where we are. My pair thinks the organism is smaller than the orb. In our journey to a shrunken state, my pair explains, we have entered a microscopic world. There is an element of the fundamental to our time after hatching. This last part silences me as I reflect on the first brain and whether we have devolved back into it.

After what seems like a long period of rumination, I respond to my pair. *Rather,* I say, *I believe that we are in a much larger space.* I felt the circumference of the orb. It did not pulse like this organism. It did not move us with such aggression. I say that *maybe we have entered the universe, one that is endless and expansive.* It is good to know there is much that is unknown. Regardless of the memories we keep from the previous worms, there is considerably more for us to absorb.

To prove a point, my pair knocks on something. It tells me so. *There is something solid,* it says. I have already tapped the material myself, curious as I am, with both ends. *It billows,* I retort. I tell my pair that we are wrapped in the fabric of the universe. This is my theory: everything is simple because we are in a larger space. It is less chaotic in this dimension. We are stuck in one of its tunnels, allowing for passage from one world to another. We only need to figure out how to move through it.

In all the time we have had in this organism, or dimension, I have focused on its makeup. I am starting to think that only I seek to be in tune with the nature of this being. In the air is an unsettling presence of nerves. A noticeable uncertainty guides its motions and fluctuations. Often, it is still. If movement is a rudimentary process of life as I have gathered, then it is in decline. Most strange of all is that the organism is routinely nourished, yet it sounds like it is gasping for air.

My pair disagrees with nearly everything I say. It is cold – *not really*. That is a loud noise – *not at all*. I think that sometimes it says things just to scare me away from thinking. My pair says that we will continue to shrink with our surroundings. Eventually we will reach a dismal size where everything will present like foam. With the other matter at this scale, we will repeatedly be created and destroyed. *Over and over*, it tells me. Over and over! It says we will lose track of each other and time. There will be no more pairs. We will become tiny specks or flecks. Each of us will float alone.

I know my pair does not believe these things. It is only stoking my fear of uncertainty out of frustration with my dreaming. It has been satisfied since we arrived. *There is food to eat and places to burrow.* My pair does not agree with me that we could find a home more like the orb. To get back at my pair, I say that being repeatedly birthed in foam sounds beautiful. Preferable, even, to drift as something so small and inconsequential.

*

In my weakest moments, I feel that where we are is not just dismal, but uninhabitable. The organism, the dimension, the universe is struggling to retain nutrients. The landscape is straining. It is only a matter of time until the organism will fail, dying, and we might die along with it. Once again, death becomes the process we are made to facilitate. The possibility of our end spreads an ache within my form, causing me to consider why I am so attached to being.

Yet there is no life I am willing to imagine for myself here. With or without my pair, I must go. Then, I will have my chance of reaching ({i}) once more. These are the thoughts I keep to myself. When I grow tired of this thinking, I imagine selfing (selfing) ((selfing)) (((selfing))) ((((selfing)))) (((((selfing))))) ((((((selfing)))))) (((((((selfing))))))) ((((((((selfing)))))))) (((((((((selfing))))))))) ((((((((((selfing)))))))))).

Passionless Decades

The worms are not passing, further asserting themselves. It is a heavy home to share. They mope about and steal Gelsomina's nutrients. In their stuttering forms, she senses the fluctuation of their serotonin levels. The little creatures have no idea that lost love is as good as any other. But who is Gelsomina to remark on love? Much of life has never happened for her.

Gelsomina has endured passionless decades, but that is not the sole reason for her emptiness. She inherited the disposition at birth. Born by the sea, she was veiled in an amniotic sac she had to break to breathe. A soft bulb syringe was used to remove fetal fluids from her throat before she was held upside down and shaken vigorously to flush out mucus. Slowly her tongue turned from blue to pink. Finally conscious, she was placed in a warm box.

Following her birth, Gelsomina was sent away in the back of a van with three other puppies. They arrived at a pet shop where they were separately locked in a wall of cages. Yelps emitted from her like an animal possessed. She was not the only one. Other dogs spent most of the day crying, though some, Gelsomina noticed, never made a peep. Over time she understood the value in keeping hushed. She enjoyed the dryness of her mouth, its gamy stench, and learned that silence was the armor of the inanimate. There were many objects in the shop that went unnoticed, and she wished to be one of them.

To the right of the wall of dogs stood terrariums with reptiles. To the left were caged brown and white mice. Burdening her most was the concoction of scents. The pet shop was a moist den stinking of the animals' relief as well as fish and dog food. At night, when the dogs were tired from howling, only the aquariums bubbled. Every morning the owner of the shop examined the dogs to choose those who would be placed in an open pen for customers to pet and hold. In those moments Gelsomina shot to the back corner of the cage, hiding her nose beneath urine-soaked newspaper. Seldom was she chosen due to her nipping and trembling.

One afternoon a woman entered the shop and examined the puppies in the pen, then those in their cages. She stopped in front of Gelsomina's cage to look at her curled figure, the spotted belly that bulged. Gelsomina shook when the door to her cage opened, and she was pulled out by her center. Yet she appreciated being held in the woman's clean arms.

The shop owner piled all the pink items available for purchase onto the counter: a circular bed, a plush blanket, a sweater, two toys, a collar, a leash, tiny boots for inclement weather, and a tote bag with a hole for her head. The woman stroked the white spots on Gelsomina's paws and chest as the items were scanned. Gelsomina was placed on the pink blanket in the passenger seat along with a stuffed strawberry holding a jovial expression. She whimpered until she exhausted herself, resting her head on the strawberry toy.

Shortly after arriving at the glass house, Gelsomina was spayed. Her hormones fluctuated in the aftermath of the surgery as though she were in heat, a cycle that completes by preparing for gestation. These changes convinced Gelsomina that she was pregnant when she was not. With the phantom pregnancy, her mammary glands enlarged, and her nipples leaked milk. She gained weight even though she was barely eating and regularly vomited.

Dogs are particularly sensitive to hormones, both their own and those produced by people. They detect subtle changes related to human pregnancy. A person using transdermal estrogen cream who touches a dog's skin can induce symptoms of a heat cycle in the animal. A phantom pregnancy occurs in about 80 percent of unspayed dogs, called *intact females*, with 67 percent experiencing recurring symptoms. In spayed dogs, a phantom pregnancy is less common. It is believed that *pseudopregnant bitches* were once helpful for a pack by protecting and feeding the young.

Rummaging through her toys despite the cone around her head, Gelsomina selected the plush strawberry from the pet shop and carried it to her bed. Her new obsession surprised the couple. She had never shown interest in the toy before. From then on, Gelsomina took the strawberry everywhere she went, even holding it in her mouth when she went out to pee. She licked the strawberry repeatedly, guarded it from the couple, and attempted to nurse it.

Symptoms typically clear up within one month. To help dissolve the phantom pregnancy, the veterinarian prescribed Galastop, a pill that inhibits the secretion of prolactin, a hormone associated with milk production and maternal behavior. The couple was directed to scold Gelsomina when she licked her mammary glands, cut down her meals to dry up her milk, and discard the strawberry toy. They were not to stroke or bathe Gelsomina. For some, the phantom pregnancy persists indefinitely, with never-ending symptoms and aggressive behavior, a condition that leads some people to euthanize their animals.

The couple struggled to ration her food when she was frequently retching. John distracted Gelsomina with a treat while Wendy confiscated the strawberry, with tears in her eyes, and tossed it in the trash can outside. Realizing the absence of her strawberry, Gelsomina whined and hoarded her toys beneath the wooden console, including a bone she once buried and dug up. Her frustration continued, culminating in her ripping open the Perron Bun Lounge Chair they had found secondhand, which, to be fair, resembled her plush ball. The veterinarian was right; Gelsomina's hormones stabilized, and her symptoms cleared within three weeks. She never had a phantom pregnancy again.

Over time, Gelsomina quietly accepted her dim life in the glass house, one that resembled the uniformity of the vast coastal landscape. Waves receded and advanced. She was destined to relive the same day. After her phantom pregnancy, there were no life events that split her open, telling her *this is how you will live now*. There was no reflex constructed for change, no fortitude against the unknown.

These days, there is little riling Gelsomina other than kibble swimming in a thin pool of water. From across the house, she smells the opening of the bag. Though the worms have ruined her appetite, Gelsomina still participates in the regular rush of the morning and afternoon meals, following at Zampanò's heels as he barrels into the kitchen.

Pieces of kibble fall from a plastic cup. The woman sets down the bowls on the floor. She squirts salmon oil into Gelsomina's bowl to encourage her appetite and make her coat shine. Gelsomina sniffs the food and leaves. She senses the woman's vexation as she places the untouched bowl of food on the counter. Sometimes she forgets to remove Gelsomina's bowl from the floor, and Zampanò finishes both meals, contributing to his surging weight.

Gelsomina is not always bored, for her anxiety about daily matters keeps her heart racing and mind alert. Certain common occurrences both stir and comfort her. A big truck arrives many mornings stinking of fish, from which three men clamber out to remove bags of garbage from the driveway. Another man, dripping sweat, runs by the front of the house, followed by a woman and her daughter walking two Standard Poodles.

Facing the street, Gelsomina gets lost in the brutality of stone. She is surprised when the picture is disrupted by the emergence of a person or animal, or when ashy plumes rise from a chimney. Even the plants are motionless. With her head on her paws, she then faces the blue sky above the glassy lake, longing for something. When she is outside, she wants to be in, and when she is inside, she wants to be out. It has been a while since Gelsomina experienced joy. It used to pour from her, drawn out by any sign of love from the woman or the man. Now, it arrives in spurts and departs just as quickly.

Wondering what it must feel like to have somewhere to go, she thinks of her own leisurely pace. Each step leaves behind a pink smudge of the blood she loosens with her tongue, caked in the fur of her front paw. It has been a long time since her last monthly wash, a chore that she makes difficult for the couple. Her loins are musky beneath the gloomy bend of her spine. Sometimes, when she forgets the reason for moving, she returns to the couch, atop a blanket she licks, overwhelmed by the haste of herself.

Gelsomina accepts that the things that happened and what she has done are the things that were meant to happen and that she was meant to do. If this were not the case, then she would not be alive and in the care of the couple. This truth props up a fragile sense of her place in the world. She navigates simple calls and responses that reveal larger patterns. There are determinants that Gelsomina names. These outcomes mean more to her than they do to others. A hat is a walk outside. The opening of a pill bottle is deli meat or cheese. A suitcase indicates departure. This last one has harmed her more than anything else.

The couple stops between their tasks to sit with Gelsomina, pacifying her with affection or food with which to administer a pill, brush her shedding fur, or wipe the crust accumulating around her eyes. Gelsomina is particularly upset when they wrench open her eyelids to dispense liquid into her pupils. This occurs at least twice per day. As she whips her head back and forth to thwart their attempts, the couple reminds her *this will only be a second*, that without the drops her eyes will swell to a size so large they might pop.

And her eyes are remarkably large for her breed. Once, Wendy swears, Gelsomina was looking up at her and when a fly landed on her eyeball, *she didn't even blink*. As Gelsomina sleeps, a sliver of each eye remains visible, sliding left to right as she navigates her subconscious.

When the drops are dispensed, Gelsomina blinks repeatedly to dispel blurred vision, transforming objects into monstrosities. She takes a nap, stimulated by anxiety and how she had been forced to hold still. Then, the kibble in the stainless-steel bowl again, around midafternoon. Since the worms arrived, she more frequently receives the same unwanted bowl of food from that morning.

Throughout the last year there are moments when Gelsomina does not recognize the man or the woman. It is not that their faces or figures are blurred, momentarily obstructed by shadows or bright light. Rather, her mind blinks. Her form responds. Gelsomina barks at the intruder, the fur on her neck rises, and her back jerks up. When they speak back to her, with laughter or in the harsh tone of annoyance, she quickly detects who they are.

Following these impasses, Gelsomina reflects on the split second when she forgot the couple and wonders about the other being who must have taken over her form. Surely, it had not been her. The same happens with Zampanò, who, during that blip in her brain, becomes a frightening animal. She growls at him until he gets close enough to sniff her face. She is soothed by the familiarity of his smell and touch and is released from her altered state.

*

Every night, the four of them split into pairs on the couch. Each dog retreats to the man or the woman, sprawling against the warmth of a thigh. News anchors lull the dogs to sleep, and the couple speaks softly of Gelsomina's sphincter, *a swollen raspberry*. They discuss allergies and worms and acknowledge with regret that she must have been rubbing her anus in circles again on their rug. Gelsomina spins in tight rings with the remaining strength of her front legs, attempting to relieve an itch so intense it is painful.

The couple considers her medicine and the balance of alleviation with the erasure of her personality. Wendy reads aloud an email from the veterinarian listing Gelsomina's many allergies: House Dust, House Dust Mites, Storage Dust Mites, Fire Ants, No-see-ums, *Alternaria Tenuis, Penicillium, Malassezia,* Bahia Grass, Johnsongrass, Redtop Grass, Perennial Ryegrass, Yellow Dock, Lamb's Quarters, Sheep Sorrel, English Plantain, Goldenrod, Cocklebur, Spiny Pigweed, Ragweed, Marsh Elder, Dog Fennel, Bayberry, Red Mulberry, Box Elder, Red Cedar, Live Oak, White Pine, Orange Trees, and Black Willows. It is a feat to keep her well.

Once the dogs' back legs are kicking, when they are whimpering from the depths of their dreams, John and Wendy retreat to their individual offices, where they read through one of the many newsletters populating their inboxes.

Other than lounging and foiling the couple's efforts to heal her, Gelsomina's tendencies are limited to the governance of her plush ball and sudden bursts of mania relinquished in short sprints down the length of the house. When she is energetic it feels as though she has returned to a younger version of herself. Front and back paws meet and shoot out again. She turns at one end of the house and makes her way back, losing speed in the process. By the time she stops, Gelsomina questions what has gotten into her. The open wound in the crease of her paw aches. The confusion about who she is frightens her more than anything. Though for that brief trot in the stretch of an empty space, she feels free.

Gelsomina notices her likeness in the shorter worm within her, who is reluctant to give even decent situations a good chance and disdains the advice and knowledge of its pair. There is little that she knows. She resents that other beings assume this about her, too, because she is constantly being tricked by what she calls *the illusions*. An example: a leaf falling from a tree appears to be a bird. Another: the woman's affection is often a precursor to the deliverance of bitter medicine. They all seem to think that she can be convinced of anything that might work in their favor.

Gelsomina keeps many secrets. She cherishes the introduction of information and things that are all her own, such as objects and games. There are items that are special to her, in addition to the plush ball, including squeakers that she has plucked from the center of toys, a clear plastic bone, and an old pair of the woman's underwear. She has kept them hidden beneath the wooden television console for years, memorizing their indentations and scents, and the sensation of the smooth squeaker that she likes best to close her mouth around. It is soft and slithers.

Now, it is the worms. Not that she likes them. They are an embarrassment, but also her own. She believes that the worms are exposing her to knowledge that even the couple cannot access. It is as though the landscape they study from within the glass house has been crafted as a miniature within her. The worms are on a grassy knoll, beside flowering bushes and rail-thin trees, a tranquil garden disrupted by their cries.

Wendy tends to include Gelsomina in the couple's relationship based on her whims. She holds Gelsomina in her lap while they engage in tiffs, methodically petting the length of her. The couple trades curt statements, and Gelsomina senses a rush of negative emotions that she is propelled to manage. It is visual, but also auditory and olfactory. It patters through both their hearts, and hers, too.

Following their conversation, Wendy places Gelsomina in a corner of the couch, arranging a fur throw over her lower half. They retreat to separate rooms where Gelsomina and Zampanò are not allowed. Wendy and John find each other later in the day to share a meal at the dining table with both dogs at their feet. There is a shift in the energy between them, and Gelsomina relaxes, sharing in their relief.

Gelsomina applies what she knows of the couple's differences to the worms. Their rows necessitate an urgent solution. And so, Gelsomina waits for the worms to break bread; for light to pierce through the inside of her and give them a proper home.

To be, Wendy once said, *implies fate; a line drawn from one to the other.* She was describing soulmates and how there can only be one. She was naming her love for John, who confirmed his line was and has always been drawn to her, rather than bifurcated, or as they have seen happen in their friends' marriages, trifurcated in the directions of others.

Does Gelsomina have a line? Rather, she orbits, and at the center of her revolutions there is no one. Her daily labors are all she wants, which are to observe the premises, subtly warn of intruders, and sleep. *To be* is unfamiliar to her in love and maternity. The worms might be her punishment, her retribution for refusing someone into her form and pushing no one out.

She seeks to learn from the worms how to love. She was never meant to. It was written out of her body at a young age. Sex has always been a duty of others. She has observed it taking place in the backyard of the glass house. For some animals, such as gray squirrels, mating looks like play in the way they chase each other up trees and once, in their exhilaration, entered the glass house through a chimney. Others, like the raccoons in moonlight, sound like they are dying in the act. The skunk is more subtle, the female burrows into a hole and waits for a mate to arrive.

Gelsomina is within the worms' love and yet separate; a carrier more than anything. At times, she enjoys being used. She is like a house or a bed. In this way, she absorbs the worms' emotions, their warm and their cold. She contributes quietly, as work should be done. Gelsomina allows a question to take shape in her mind about the stories she tells herself about her body. Is there yearning? During moments of rage while following the soft orange light of a fox, a creature that stalks the property of the glass house, she feels an urge near where the worms now live. It is an impulse to go forward, confusing rage with longing.

A sharp, almost painful feeling bubbles up in her abdomen. Sometimes it wraps around her and releases itself in short, thrusting motions against her plush ball. There is something about this physical expression that the couple dislikes, prompting them to tell her to *stop*. Perhaps it is her individuality that bothers them. *That was all,* Gelsomina thought of her propulsions to intimacy, *that was all.*

Though she has spent many afternoons beside a felled tree with a calendar embalmed in its center, Gelsomina has never considered herself within a broader sense of history. She is only beginning to understand how time impresses itself on one's form. And what is love but the desecration of time, its simultaneous expansion and contraction, the feeling that decades have been marshaled into a few weeks? The opposite is also true, so that many years together can lead to interactions between strangers.

Gelsomina has a conception of love as an entity that warps and solves problems. She keeps tabs on the worms' relationship like a new mother and her sleeping baby. From her limited perspective, she most wants the worms to lay orbs within her as the exemplary symbol of their union. Each being both male and female, they are to wrap and touch head-to-end, head-to-head, and end-to-end. They will connect at their centers, enveloped in mucus. But the worms have been communicating less. They have been touching less. The worms have removed themselves from each other.

Newborn Choir

It is not that I will just become everything in this house. Rather, I am a self-sexing being holding two fruiting organisms. Contrary to belief, I am gestating for the smallest, who are hidden and cruel. I am not certain how the twain creatures found me. A dispersion of the waterbody, or are they a manifestation of my form? My lumpen last act. Thousands of apple seeds must rest within me, sprouting an orchard. Bacterium singing my leaves. Codling moths in the cankers of my limbs, proliferating once thawed. The blue-eyed monsters fire at the tips of their wings. After a life of hibernation, my chilled dormancy enables a bloom of white and pink, an expression of actuality I did not ask for. Though I might very well have been punished for my prior latency because those who matter are those who produce and reproduce. But if beings make reproductions, then the original being must be a production. There was nothing else for me to do. That long time before the twain creatures my only task was to exist, though I did not do that well. I was a sorry remnant of sorts. The trench in my gut recalls my sole creation, prior to the pasteurization of the glass house. I did not give birth but young appeared. It was following a blackout and my return in agony. The stitching of my abdomen marking a clear barrier. And a plastic sphere wrapped around my head preventing my grip on things. Then, a progeny erected as a pink misshapen ball. Nothing like me. One who would not wake nor eat but nonetheless existed. I suckled my little. I nursed my little who would not nurse. I carried my little to water and air. Motionless – but when I pressed my little, it squeaked. I prodded my little for weeks. I listened for changes in the squeak, greedy for new squeaks. Then, distracted by the raw scent of glutinous consumption, I turned back and my little was gone. Feet shuffling of the conditional. Scent tracing in the consequence of glory. Evidence of a sea wind knocking sacs of those who are not yet. Buoyant stupidity of the unGod! My *little*. I gathered all the things that had been suggested were mine. Ramshackled under the wooden console. I who have nothing; I who am nothing. Regardless of this past, I must now count, too, and be given my honor for the work of supporting others – as a product of mother and father who has now become both mother and father? Who produces more mothers and fathers to become mothers and fathers? Singular/plural/conjoined. For me: fission. The creation of many from one. They are taking pieces of me in the process, including a false sense of possession and the idea that my form is my own belonging. Here I am condemned to raising the ones who are killing me. Fungus eating animal matter. I am matter. I matter at least as the being who sits in this spot and occupies this air. A corner is all I ask for. One with enough space to turn around and choose to face a quiet surface. Instead, every corner is a window, and place is infinite. The horizon knocks on the doors. How big it all could be makes me ill. It appears mostly to be the original out there. Oh, what do *I* know? Everything is rife with imitation in the glass atmosphere. False stone and wood. I am an imitation, too, suckling on the translucent orb of a dead plush object, which is meant to be its heart. Instead of pulsing, the organ shrieks, not unlike my little. The plush object was given to me by the man. It resembles a branch, but with fur and reeking of his tobacco like the inside of his vehicle. The morning he gave it to me, I shook the object mad. I shook it mad and ripped it open, revealing its limited proof of existence. One by one I removed white tufts from within the object that made it full and real. I dragged around its empty form. Now, I hold its perpetual heart in my mouth. I knock the wind out of it. Rubber, hollow. I concentrate on its howling nipple. If only I could press its middle and lick its nipple at the same time, then I would wholly understand it. Lost in my spasms, the quick repetition of face to heart and face to heart – suddenly the woman slips it out from under me. She pulls the heart away, holding its wet and dirtied structure, a transparent moon, by her two fingers, signaling me to stop. *No*, she says. As if I could continue without this heart. It has to do with my own descent to an end, my curiosity. I need something still and whole like this for me to learn the mechanisms of my reality. I swaddle the rubber heart in fear but wonder if it could ever really die. In fits of rage and misunderstanding, I have tried to kill the heart. It is unpierceable, unsmashable, the heart is regurgitant. It flows in the direction opposite of mine. It has a different time. And if I were to consume the plush object's heart, it might reside within me for good. Then, following my end, the object's heart will be removed from my form, and the process will repeat. I believe that at the end of life there is a spore ready to feed on the last of what can be given by my form. A minuscule but important reminder that even the thing that cannot be denied by others – physical presence – will be stolen from me. I have seen the dead insects and birds, a squirrel and one iridescent fish. When my time comes, I will tell the spore who is not so visible: I am from a sac or a hand, the liver or lungs. I am blue or green. I have learned I am more than a couch. More than actions spurred by the gestures of others and the recipient of best guesses. This is the first clear awakening in the disturbed patch of my mind. The controlled hallucination of my end. A hungry spore and an eternal heart. Fog dissipates and though I am getting bigger, holding more, so is this house. Ever-elongating expanses. Brutalist stretches. The sky appears on a mock ceiling. Here I am in a corner. Beside me is the houseplant. It is locked within a rough and scratchy confinement. Rejected water pools at its base. Moisture/shade/acidity. Faintly, its high-pitched scream. Then, popping noises of agony as it drowns. The barrier is slim between the houseplant and the branches of the tree tickling on the other side. The original thrives as the elevated home of raccoons and squirrels. Under the flat plains of its leaves, I smell disease in the potted soil. When I am this close to the houseplant, air rapidly enters me and my horn honks. I have difficulty breathing. Sometimes I make these unexpected noises and afterward press again, repeatedly, the object's circular heart. If I were taller, I would rip out a stalk of the plant and walk it through the house as a parade of our shared silent delusion, the strained belief that we have something to offer. Instead, we both exhibit a malaise the result of this stale air. Today I am silent, thinking. All this time and just now an awakening? Before, I reflected the couple. A poor simulation of human desire. It must be the first moment I have truly questioned me. What makes me. Are the twain creatures bringing these thoughts to me? Their gestures pepper my environment alongside the voices of the couple. The worms kick in wee motions. The couple stands together in the kitchen frying a meal that reeks of flesh I want to eat. Another woman's voice sings, and there is steam dissipating from a pot. One could wonder if she is stuck in there. All the emerging artificial voices are high pitched or low. Cacophony of real-life pattering. No matter, the house hog rests easy in an armchair. Chest rising and falling, air vibrating against the flattened skull. How serene, though this house is encroaching. Controlling figure determining where and how we go. It is not just the surface. Everything is porous. Yet we are all stopped short. Lurking beneath are propelling molecules. I feel them resist me and here I am, immovable. I am the outlier. Death specter, ground of toxic life. The couple smells it on me, death. They must. I know it in the hesitancy of their touch. In the hierarchy of our order. What time I am suddenly makes a difference. As though, in the same way, we all understand and abide by the same time. As though our existences are at all comparable. In this way, my prescribed surroundings tiptoe around me, doubting, assuming, calculating my remaining revolutions. Holding and rejecting. From here, in a corner with a heart in my mouth, I watch the couple embrace. I see their lightness, their hue of peach, telling me they do not know of the spore. That they will split and encounter the spore on their own one day. That they have not prepared for the spore, a *lower* plant that perseveres in unfavorable conditions for long periods of time. Central unit capable of becoming anyone. This history was learned from the houseplant. It relayed a truth that was not so different from the crackling of the detached screens populating this house. Prophets from the outside. I resent the couple's ease in coming and going amid the pandemonium they have allowed here. I wonder if the twain creatures have stirred this restlessness and fury within me. My internal mouth has opened wide in my hidden space. Our newborn choir. The questions arrive with a fierceness, and I respond with rigor. My form, debilitated, only providing use for the twain creatures. It has receded to consider itself. How I lie perfectly still. How I let the waves wash over me. There is the rising tide. Like: are there versions of me that are purer than this contained one here? Versions without the nomenclature of this glass structure? *House* dog. *House* man. *House* woman. *House* worms? A purer existence for myself. I am not even sure what that could mean. Perhaps useful, out there, but I cannot imagine what my use could be either. As a product, or production, I was supposed to be already *being*. No requirement for duplications or copies. It is all so uncertain. For the first time there is the possibility of other experiences for me. Also, for the first time, there are two landscapes: within me and in front of me. Really, three: within me, in front of me, and beyond me. I am unsure how they can all exist simultaneously. Elemental rendition of me and the twain creatures. I rely on the object's heart to still my own. It is an anchored boat in my pooling saliva. I am thinking differently about the very basics of my essence. Every breath and every lap is fuel for the twain creatures. They speak of my pending end. Even my spit belongs to them. Could I say the same of the man and the woman? Once, maybe. Though now I cannot say they are interested in my form. Invested, but no longer curious nor engaged. Examining more than touching, analyzing more than binding. Somehow, they still do not know of the twain creatures. Perhaps because the twain creatures are an invasion that has not yet grown – they are still only twain. One seeks reproduction. Creating more of exactly what they are. They inform me of the millions of fingers within me, the tentacles, and the obstacles that I come with. They remind me that I have little to offer. They wind through my orchard in darkness. When an apple is released from a branch, the ground and the apple move toward each other. I have been thinned by the tree, dropped due to my overripe nature. Here I am rotting, the twain creatures, my soon-to-be-sprouting seeds. I must be complicit. And where are the other tangled facts of my existence that have gone unknown? My inhibited perception – whose fault is that? I hear the horizons knocking. The worms, young and feral, buck around, wanting a response from me. It would be much easier to reach my end. I wish for my end. What to do with fallen apples and new blooms. Separately, why does the apple fall and not the sun or moon? And what about this heart? I hear it shriek once more. These are the secrets that I did not know were hidden. A sense of disequilibrium as everything falls toward all others falling.

~~

There is no peace because there is no light. Forward and backward have no meaning. Vibrations are muted. Through my pores everything tastes acidic. I have never been constricted like this, emotionally. I worry how long we will last here. The other worm, who will only refer to me as *my pair*, a term of union it claims is inherited – it is difficult to share our differences. Whereas I want to reproduce, expanding our reach and control of this organism, the other worm is looking to return to the orb. It cannot handle the realities of this organism.

I am not optimistic and so I focus on the small things within my control. Every day they get smaller. I keep myself centered on one point because we have found it is impossible for us to move in tandem. The other worm canvasses the organism with such vigor. At times, there is nothing to grip and our elongated forms slide. My only hope is that the place does not become too moist, that we do not drown in ignorance. I wish to stick my head into these walls, for us to attach and remain still. As a side effect of our hatching together, our early attachment, there is a part of me that desperately wants this other worm to reach well-being.

I am running out of patience. I do not mean to be unfair, but the other worm is sure that we have entered a space like the sky, even though we can feel the walls, even though we cannot go in straight lines.

I have conceded by saying that we are shrinking. If the other worm considered my point, a belief I manufactured, it would understand that eventually both of our statements would be correct. We will have shrunk to such a small size that we will be in a space that mimics the sky. These conversations are futile. In other words, there is no point in arguing where we are. We simply need to *be* where we are.

Throughout the other worm's philosophizing, it has been my responsibility to manage the health of our host, and tailor our responses accordingly. If we take too much of its nutrients, the immune count of the organism will decrease and its chances for survival will diminish. In this animal's morbid defeat, the other worm freely takes as it mimes on about finding another orb. I have been wondering if there is another environment within this animal that will satisfy the other worm. We could move north to higher ground. A drier atmosphere might prevent its runoff ideas. Perhaps light will trickle in, or we could find another host altogether. I would only consider this last option after exhausting all others.

The other worm, on top of pontificating, is preoccupied with the idea of ({i}). It is an energy I was born believing in, too; an entity I also encountered while inside the orb. But I am not wrapped up in the possibilities of its meaning. I do not claim it as my own. My understanding is that this figure appears to all beings who enter the universe. For the other worm it is a symbol of belief, one that dictates how life should be lived. The other worm attempts to unravel its code by evaluating the moments when ({i}) arrived in our orb, and in turn tells me how we should be acting to entice the figure once again.

Since the beginning, we have disagreed on how we are meant to use our forms. It is the crack we cannot mend, the chasm between each other that we will never cross. I am set on the proliferation of ourselves, and an ongoing symbiosis with the host that we have been offered. The other worm explicitly stands by an existence shaped by the presence and absence of illumination. It seeks pleasure in revolutions and expanse in a place without barriers. It communicates the ultimate destination, a revelatory state of ({i}). The other worm tells me that our time in the orb made clear that a better way of being is out there, without articulating where *there* might be.

The endless rapture of its engagement with the orb and ({i}) weighs on me. Some things will never be clear. We might have the answers we are looking for already within our forms. As in, we were born with the solutions. Time rattles forward unintelligibly here, without indication or warning, requiring our focus. Chaos can only be met with ordinary attempts at routine. I have begun mine, a rotation of critical tasks: evaluating the health of the animal, feeding myself, ensuring the safety of the other worm, and considering our journey.

In spare moments, a certain horror seizes me. I become numb to sensation and hand myself over to a void. The feeling is departure, yet I am nowhere. Surroundings become thin and vaporous. A recurring thought arrives that we are sick creatures, that deep inside us is a thing inherently wrong. I suppose this is the root of how the other worm and I differ. The other worm believes this environment is bad, whereas I believe the fault lies within us and will be taken wherever we go. With this, stasis disturbs me. Action is my only remedy. I tell this to the other worm, who in turn darts off to the place of rest for the dead who hatched with us. It curls by their empty forms and raps both its ends on the surface before them. It vibrates the fluids within its tube to stimulate our surroundings and awaken the dead. It is a ritual I refuse to acknowledge.

And – I cannot avoid it – there is one thing that I have trouble even whispering about in my thoughts. The other worm returns to the idea of killing our host. It tells me that the only way forward begins with starting over. Who are *we* to determine whether this animal lives? The willingness of the other worm to end a life worries me. What else might it do on a whim? Could the other worm kill me? Does the other worm *seek* to kill me? These questions are nauseating and send me spinning. I count my segments to quell my mind, as a gentle reminder that I exist here.

I have been considering life with another worm. There must be other orbs that took this passage, traveling farther than or not as far as we have, and hatching at least two good worms. Is it so illicit that I seek a reiteration of myself in both form and philosophy? To search for another worm will be a silent quest veiled by my desire for a new location. The path will be shared. The other worm continues to thrust itself against these walls, a cry for any solution to the relentless dark. I cannot leave this worm behind.

The Fox

It snuck up on her – the need to know where the fox had been. The urge unfolded gradually. Gelsomina remembers the first day she saw the fox from her place on the living room couch. A creature, like her in size with a brilliant coat, passed through the yard, slowed to a trot, then lodged itself in the lavender bushes. The fox has a sharp nose and ears, and an enormous tail. A perfume scent comingles with its musk.

Since contracting the worms, Gelsomina's interest in the striking creature has grown. It is the fox's color, emerging as flashes of orange, that impels her search. Or perhaps it is the fox's fur, long and coarse, that draws Gelsomina to look for it between the trees. It is difficult for her to understand the feeling. For the first time, she wishes to sink her face into an outside creature's form, to place it in the available position of her plush ball.

The chance to catch even a snippet of its ginger coat has Gelsomina doing things that she would have never done before, such as lying in the sun for many hours. She wants to see if stillness pacifies the fox, encouraging it to traipse through the property once more. The feeling is like an animal roaming inside her in search of water, a type of agony she has not felt since her early days with the couple. She is reminded of the ferocity of herself, a stubborn nature that prevents her from acting with clarity.

Gelsomina rarely sees the fox. Her cataractous eyes follow the sun's trick orange light until she reaches water. A mock fox tail drags itself down the center of the lake. This optical illusion happens regularly. She turns her attention to the nearby bushes of leather flowers where she hears rustling. It is usually a squirrel, or a few small birds.

Today, she stops to smell a scent that is not her own. She can tell the sex of the animal, its reproductive status, whether it was stressed upon urinating, its sicknesses, and what time it passed through the yard. Yet she does not know what to do with this information. Gelsomina urinates out of routine. To do so relaxes her, as though boundaries are being drawn between her and the wandering animals, between her and that of the untold.

What would happen if she and the fox crossed paths? Gelsomina cannot arrive at an answer. There is no version of herself who would engage with the fox in a way that does not involve fear. Back inside, having given up and retreated to the familiarity of the glass house, she hears the foxes' calls late into the night. One howls and barks. A vixen lets loose a bloodcurdling squeal.

Around the world there are phrases used for the surprise of rainfall on a sunny day. Depending on where someone is located, they might hear the following English translations to describe the natural phenomenon: the devil is getting married; pineapple rain; the hyena is giving birth; the devil is kissing his wife; the witch is combing hair; the wolf is giving birth on a mountain; the groom is eating unheated food; the poor are getting married; the jackal's wedding; a wedding is being celebrated in Hades; the rabbit is giving birth, the witch is making butter; the witches are making soft bread. In Japan, one might hear that the fox is taking a wife, or that it is the fox's wedding. The trickster fox summons the rain to keep others away so that he can wed his bride in a private ceremony. The phrase also refers to atmospheric ghost lights, which appear in the sky as an omen that someone is going to die.

Historically in literature, the fox is a sly and cunning animal, a con artist who generates mischievous schemes to which others fall prey. The fox would not likely wander onto the property of the glass house as Gelsomina hopes. The animal is too strategic, with a keen sense of direction. Like deer and cattle, the fox aligns itself with the earth's electromagnetic field, using it as a targeting system to measure its distance from prey. A chicken thief and master hunter, the fox would only enter the property of the glass house with reason. Gelsomina, who was too large to eat, was not one of those reasons.

The following morning, Gelsomina wants to be let out again. Though she is racked with ailments, and the sunny day broken by light rainfall, she heaves herself up from clotted blankets and wanders over to the back door. She watches the property, waiting for the man or the woman to relinquish her. They do so without thinking, hoping that she will relieve herself outside rather than in.

Gelsomina steps onto the stone patio overlooking the vast and reflective surface of the lake. She filters for the scent that is the most meaningful – the sweet urine of the fox. Gelsomina takes her time to find and follow the fox's path around the yard. In doing so, she drags her nose across the soil, but does not drink standing water, as she has done many times before, in fear of garnering additional worms.

In the process of meandering, Gelsomina grows lost in the vibrations of plants and animals. She has always heard their murmurings when she leaves the glass house; the chattering of rodents and insects; a distant hum arrives through the soil. Occasionally a plant screams. Rarely has she been addressed. A baby deer once marveled at Gelsomina's corrugated snout. A bee landed and buzzed in her ear then stung her biting mouth. She listens closely as she walks across one length of the property, remaining a conscientious stretch from the Invisible Force.

For the first decades of her life, every sound or smell was an affront. Gelsomina crushed leaves, kicked up dirt, and ate bugs. She chased squirrels, chipmunks, lizards, and birds. As she has aged and calmed, the path from the house to the water has gone through little change. The seasons dress and undress the trees. The ground softens with rainfall and hardens with sunlight.

Gelsomina falls into a rhythmic walk behind Zampanò's urgent tumble into the landscape. She sniffs for the fox at the base of trees and presses into the imprints of its paws, before stopping to lie down at the shoreline. She studies the water. Out of the corner of her eye, Gelsomina sees a worm flitting across the soil. Another appears covered in dew. They slither on damp earth, wrapping around each other.

It is not the first time Gelsomina has seen the worms, but they do not show themselves every day. The last time she came upon worms birthed from their orbs, Gelsomina had been walking aimlessly along the water tasting bitter red soil when a harsh wind brushed against her face, prompting her to pause. It was around three in the afternoon, and the sequence arrived to her as a nativity scene. Gelsomina witnessed twenty lovers, or ten pairs of worms. Without meaning to, Gelsomina imagined all twenty of them in her mouth and, ill with the feeling of their glazed forms between her teeth, she turned to leave.

These worms are surrounded by debris. She cannot know if they are the same species of worms as her own. They look too big to be inside of her, and the vision makes her queasy. The worms halt, sensing Gelsomina, then lose interest and float on a water surface littered with insects and petals. The appearance of the first pair reveals many others cradled by algae or exasperated beside rotten raspberries. They leap and curl like dancers, spontaneously somersaulting onto the grass. They compare the purple ends of their tubular forms before bucking back into the water.

A Bad Omen

A worm's bile is said to be the material that was combined with water to create the world. Intimacy with a creator does not make worms inherently good, though some worms are. They contribute to the regeneration of soil that can be tilled to produce food. Globally, people have bought parasitic worms and worm eggs online, which are shipped in glass vials and used to treat a variety of health conditions such as depression, leading to the evaluation of pig whipworm eggs as an ingredient for sale in Germany. Other worms, masked by their size, convince people of their inferiority, only to later take control of their bodies and land.

Encountering a worm is not the best omen. Across cultures, worms are said to foretell the future and mark a point in time before great change. A well-known tale tells the story of a worm found by a seamstress within an apple, which she fed milk, rice, and honey. The worm grew to an enormous size and brought goodwill to a city of people. Its role as a beneficiary did not last long. Soon it was clear that the worm sought to take over as ruler of all surrounding regions. In anticipation of the usurper, a nobleman got the keepers of the worm drunk, snuck into its cage, and killed the worm with a sword.

Another worm in another town, lurking beneath the surface of a body of water, was caught by a fisherman then thrown back into its habitat. The worm returned to the fisherman's town seven years later after having grown as large as a house. It wrapped itself around a central hill. After many attempts by the townspeople to remove the worm, it took the strength of the original fisherman to kill it. Today, there are seven marks on the hill where the grass does not grow, but white mushrooms do, creating what is called a fairy ring.

Worms can be found in every environment on the planet, including harsh ones like the harrowing Antarctic waters. Most worms breathe through their skin and have one or two holes to eat and defecate. Though they are known for having soft and slender forms with no limbs, there are worms with a stump called a *parapodium* to help them walk. Comically, there is a pigbutt worm, or the flying buttocks, which looks as it is named, floats midwater, glows in the dark, and turns blue when touched.

In one acre of land there can be more than one million worms. For every human on the planet, there are an estimated 60 billion nematodes. Some marine worms share 70 percent of human genes, a higher percentage than a comparison of humans to chickens. The *C. elegans* worm, which is the size of a human hair, has the smallest brain known to man, and its neurons are shockingly like those found in the human brain. There are some worms whose eyes are twice the width of their bodies. Others carry their own parasites.

Two roundworms that had been buried in the ice for 46,000 years were thawed in water and found still living, exemplifying the ability for life to be put on pause and later restarted. The two female worms lived out their lifespan of a few days by reproducing in the lab. Similarly, seeds buried in Siberian permafrost were thawed 32,000 years later, growing into many *Silene stenophylla* with delicate white flowers.

There are thin Gordian worms named for their ability to tie themselves in a knot. They belong to a small phylum called the *Nematomorpha*, meaning the form of a thread. They look like a thin shoelace that has been left behind, or a strand of cooked spaghetti. When they are tied up, they resemble a golden necklace that has been carelessly tossed into a jewelry box, requiring patient unraveling. Great numbers of Gordian worms appear after rainfall, convincing people that the worms fell from the sky, or that they are horsehairs that have landed in a pond and come to life. The nominally adjacent ribbon worm emits a proboscis, or a retractable organ that captures prey.

A sixty-four-year-old woman from New South Wales was admitted to the hospital after suffering abdominal pain, diarrhea, a fever, night sweats, a dry cough, forgetfulness, and depression. After reviewing an unusual MRI scan, a neurosurgeon pulled an eight-centimeter-long parasitic roundworm, still alive and writhing, from her brain. The worm was sent to an expert at the Commonwealth Scientific and Industrial Research Organisation, who identified the parasite as *Ophidascaris robertsi*, commonly found in pythons. The woman lived in an area infested with pythons, and though she did not interact with them, she used native grasses in her cooking. The team believed that the woman had consumed the pythons' feces, and along with it, the larvae of the parasitic worms.

On the site of Stonehenge, ancient feces revealed that the builders of the monument were infected with parasitic worms after eating a feast of raw meat. In Texas, there are worms with the same head as a hammerhead shark that emerge from the soil after it rains. In Connecticut, a creature described as *an earthworm on steroids* put the state's forest ecosystem under threat by ruining the soil and killing local plant life. They even toppled stone walls. Officials encouraged residents to use vinegar or dish soap to kill the worms themselves. In Florida, sand flies attack beachgoers' legs, transmitting flesh-eating parasites through bites that turn into open wounds. As temperatures rise, the invisible could proliferate, cascading through food systems and into new regions. Environmental stresses make beings more susceptible to parasites seeking a host, spiking the rate of transmission.

No matter the type of worms you have contracted, you will be treated in the same way. The doctor will test a sample of your feces. Medicine will be self-administered for one to three days. The worms will eventually exit with a bowel movement, sometimes visibly so. To avoid contracting worms in the future, hosts are advised to wash their hands frequently, drink filtered water, avoid walking barefoot on soil, and not eat raw or undercooked freshwater fish and meat.

One can worm their way into a scenario or situation, implying they did so dishonestly. It is understood as a devious act by a previously trusted person. A person can also worm their way out of a situation, usually one that is undesirable, similarly using a clever excuse. In Old English, *wyrm* was a much broader term, encompassing reptiles, serpents, and dragons, and later incorporating the earthworm. Less common definitions of *worm* include the nautical act of making a rope smooth, and in computing, a program that propagates itself.

God sent a worm to Jonah to save him from a *vine-centered life*. Meaning, an existence that was centered around material objects rather than the God who was gifting them.

It is believed that worms confront beings who are feeling invisible, challenging them to look within themselves and find their inner truth. This search is paired with a quest in the physical world. The worm symbolizes death and rebirth, and spiritual enlightenment through an endless renewal of life.

My Pair

The worms' existence within Gelsomina has not been easy. Time, at first urgent, is now upended. It has a new order, too. They have learned the modes of Gelsomina's rest, from her lucid dreaming to a deep slumber. Unlike her, the worms do not operate on a twenty-four-hour schedule divided by waking and sleeping. They slept between the larval stages of their development and are now permanently awake.

It is during her heavy sleeps that the worms move around. There is a top, a bottom, and two sides. All are continuous – a tube. Moving in either direction, the worms come across a segment like a warning. The worms never cross the line together. One stays in place as an anchor, while the other moves past the line and reports that there is only much more of the same. The one who stays behind sends out vibrations for its pair to follow. Occasionally one of the worms will lie, keeping a discovery to itself, which is never profound. These findings include a strange bump or an exceptionally acidic spot.

One of the worms grumbles about feeling weak, while the other tries to make a comfortable home. Mostly they weigh trouble, as in which route will bring more of it. The worms go in circles, both literally around the diameter of Gelsomina's small intestine, but also figuratively in their discussions. The endpoint of this circle of conversing, also a beginning, is the reality that the worms have not yet reproduced. Therefore, they will not have offspring who travel through the feces of the dying animal to then infect others.

Are they living out their purpose? And if not? There is not much to turn their attention to other than the absence of the orb. There are their own forms, which pulse arrhythmically, and their host, near yet out of reach. The question of what they are doing if not reproducing has become a question of who they are. Without the language for this conundrum, the worms are questioning the i of their ({i}). Perhaps this is why one of the worms is not comfortable in a place of darkness, for it must face i so directly, without the distraction of sensorial beauty and the insinuation of color throughout the illuminated stretch of a day.

Years before, Wendy and John visited an art museum to see James Turrell's *Hind Sight (Dark Space)*. They walked side by side down a dark hallway, holding on to railings attached to the walls, and into a pitch-black space. The railings ended at two chairs: plush at the top and seat, with wooden arms. They felt the contours of the chairs to sit down, then took in darkness. They were just far enough from each other to not be able to touch. It takes fifteen minutes for the rods in the eyes to adapt to the dark room, the time at which the experience ends.

The couple believed that they could see the shape of the room, but as soon as it solidified, it morphed. They must have been facing a wall. And at the bottom of the wall, there was light. Yes, there was a blank wall directly across from them and at its bottom was a soft, white light. It seemed that there were no other chairs in front of them. It was only the wall. And the ground — one of them rubbed their shoes across its textured surface — carpet.

Wendy spoke and it startled John. Should they be speaking? Somehow the inability to see made it feel as though the air was thinning. And if one of them were to leave? 'I want to leave,' Wendy said. 'No, stay,' John responded. If one were to leave, they would have to maneuver to find the railing, and make their way alone back down the hallway, which was not straight but required bumping into sharp turns to arrive back at the well-lighted gallery space. They stayed.

The white light was an illusion, for it then rose to the ceiling, becoming a flower. For John, an abstract painting. They both knew that it was a fabrication of their minds and not part of the exhibit, because one of them would have mentioned the bending white light. The exhibit description would not have said this was an experience of darkness. There were noises that seemed unintentional, the footsteps and voices fumbling overhead, and they wondered if this bothered the artist.

They breathed in through the nose and out through the mouth. Their bodies calmed. At last, they were comfortable. Thoughts arrived and left, though they were not memorable. The artwork seemed to be about darkness — *I guess.*

Then, they rose and left. They held railings, tripping over their own feet. Light trickled in with every step. There was the guard. There was the line of other people waiting to experience darkness. As they walked to the next room to take a seat on a bench, Wendy and John could not remember why they had left. They did not even know if they had stayed for the full fifteen minutes.

Had a bell rung telling them their time was up? Maybe a beep, because that is much less intrusive and easy to forget, considering how many things in their lives are constantly beeping. Had one of them stood, so the other followed? 'You stood first,' Wendy said. John chuckled. 'I don't think I did.' Or had they begun to see?

The noises the worms hear, such as the trickling of water and humming, are not much different from those they heard on the other side of their orb. These comparisons give them the language for regret, which is all that is needed to elude happiness. A question that one worm returns to, and that the other says is unproductive, is whether they are truly inside another animal.

Just as people muse that they are living in a simulation, the worms debate whether they are locked in a cave by the water rather than within another organism. The walls do not feel like rock, but damp, pulsing leather. *It is strange*, one worm ponders, *our orb rolled into the water, and then we were suddenly enveloped in a shadow. Yet when we hatched, we were no longer in water.* The place is altogether much more substantial. They deliberate whether they were not born after all and are living an afterlife. Perhaps they are being punished for the deaths of the three other worms. Once it sinks in again that they are stuck, the shorter worm grows desperate. Its tiny ends knock against Gelsomina's insides.

The information the worms have at their disposal does not always make sense, though these peculiarities are accepted as facts of life. An example is their knowledge of the intricate history of worms and stones. Along the waterbed, stones have been the setting through which worms interact with their fossilized ancestors. Their ribbed bodies are encased in white on the flat plane of a rock. Living worms curl within the indentations. Often there are imprints of two worms resting side by side.

In a moment of silence, tuckered out from rapping on Gelsomina's organs, they consider whether they are experiencing the transformation from flesh to stone. Perhaps if they embody the solid form, they will be allowed to return to the surface of the earth, encased in a hard, sculptural rendition of their orb. Together, they will roll. It will not be the end of their lives, but a new way of living. They yearn for the stability of a rock form. *We envy the stone; we envy the stone.* To bring forth this reality, one worm tells the other all the things it knows of the stone: *it is concrete, and so are its thoughts; it started as a mountain before the elements carved it down; stone measures the age of the earth.*

Leaving *Hind Sight* without a cue could only mean one of two things: there was an indication of ending, or their bodies were so in sync that they both knew it was time to depart. Wendy and John concluded that they had risen simultaneously, that it had been a twinned action. At that point their minds and bodies had accepted the anxiety that arose with the artwork. The hallucinatory attempts to give shape to their surroundings were complete. Instead, a relaxed settling into the chair, but also nothingness. Did it bother them that they never knew the room?

At lunch, to finish off the debate, they looked online for the reactions of others to the piece, finding no mention of a change that had occurred. It was always that way, dark and senseless until the rods kicked in and there was a blurry blue idea of objects in place, which one user boasted had happened for him well before the fifteen-minute mark.

Reluctant, without any finality, they discussed how most imaginings occur in the dark. There are optical illusions, tricks of the body, but it is also where one dreams, reflects on the past, and hypothesizes short- and long-term futures. One envisions the inside of their own body as the heartbeat laps against the chest and rings in the ears, the stomach gurgles, sighs erupt into the room, and the other ways in which what enters must at some point exit.

The long worm pleads that they must stop trying to uncover the meaning of their situation. The short worm, who is done with entertaining the hypothetical realities of their surroundings, retorts that it is too somber to do anything. The long worm has grown restless and frustrated with its shorter pair. Here they are, alive, together, and its pair can only speak of its birth. Some beings hatch unhappy and stay that way.

The worm's pondering, ranting, and crying continues for days. Each of its five hearts pump blood through two throbbing vessels. It worries that if they cannot reach the surface, the pores across their forms will constrict and suffocate. Until, one morning, the worms wake with their heads interlocked as if they suddenly remembered each other. Entangled, one whispers to the other: *my pair*. They take turns telling stories of a time when creatures held raspberries overhead.

The Fetus Is a Parasite

Gelsomina catches Wendy's or John's eye as they walk by, questioning whether they are going to administer more medicine. She can tell by their slow sheepishness when they are going to do so. This time, they evaluate Gelsomina's stare, wishing to be recognized, as Wendy stalls an empty hand before her mouth for her to sniff or lick. With no response from Gelsomina, she pets from the top of her head down to her tail.

When Gelsomina turns her foggy gaze back to the glass, Wendy and John wonder aloud to each other about what she could be watching outside. This type of staring is different from her old ways, they agree, because it is empty and without meaning. They look outside to see what she sees. They think of what it might be like to have all that free time – *and do what?* They often say they envy their dogs' lives.

'She's probably like this because I gave her a full allergy pill instead of half like usual,' Wendy says.

Wendy recalls the side effects listed on the bottle: drowsiness, dizziness, and double vision. A chipmunk scurries across the yard, and Wendy points as it perches on a rock, paws clasped and resting beneath the chin. They watch the animal for a moment, then return to the subject of Gelsomina's state of mind. Once all her ailments have been picked up and set down, the couple transitions to the topic of the glass house, having been brought so close to its glass-ness.

'You notice the glass when you're standing beside it, but when you're sitting on the couch it feels private in here,' Wendy says. She brings her hand to the window then just as quickly pulls it away so as not to leave a mark. 'But I feel exposed when I'm watching TV and a delivery person waves to me when they drop off a package.' This is a conversation that the couple has had numerous times.

'Well, that person and especially them waving breaks down any idea of privacy,' John says. The couple is still entertaining the idea of renovating the exterior of the glass house.

'Later, I'll show you the precedents I pulled the other day,' John says. He studies the water and adds, 'I read an article this morning about how invasive bamboo is.' He points to a miniature fence of the stubborn plant at the edge of the yard. 'These people had bamboo on their property, and it was so strong that it grew through their foundation and out the oven.'

'Do you think that could happen to us?' Wendy asks, eyeing the appliances.

'It's really hard to get rid of, but I don't think so,' John says.

Stirring Gelsomina out of her daydream, Wendy grabs her by her center and carries her over to the sectional couch. She plops Gelsomina on top of a blanket, positioning her as she usually likes, down the length of a thigh. Knowing that touch now upsets her, Wendy picks up the remote and turns on the television while keeping her lower body still.

After a few minutes, Gelsomina licks her jowls and stands. The stench of rotten food wafts from her teeth into the air. She walks over Wendy's lap to a far corner of the couch, where she digs into the blankets, turns in two circles, and lies down. She watches Wendy from across the room without blinking her infinite, black eyes.

The worms stir questions in Gelsomina about how the glass house has buffered her from the realities of her anatomic form. Her purpose throughout her long life has always been to be by the couple's side, and the couple's purpose has been to be by hers. This is how it is and always has been: food, water, touch, run, ball, sleep, curl, squeaker, the woman's underwear, heat, outside, and plastic bone. And it has always been the same.

One worm is adamant about the proliferation of their forms, and the obsession with the act fascinates her, then the lack of patience for offspring. She considers the moment when the worms will scan a landscape of orbs of their own making. The couple has not reproduced, either, to her knowledge. It is as though the glass house has its own set of laws. The structure insinuates sterility. It is an observatory, a strict bulwark preventing reproductive intimacy.

While pursuing a relationship between her and the couple, she evaded her own chances at love. She wants what the couple has without her, though it feels like an endeavor that is more so something she *should* do than one she is compelled to do. It is a want born out of woeful feelings; envy, but also the sense that her life has strayed from an intended path. Gelsomina cannot conjure up who or what determines a being's path.

There are not many potential suitors for Gelsomina in the glass house. Zampanò is out of the question. He is too bumbling and brutish for her taste, too young and wrapped up in the sentimentality of life. And what would he want with her? She is nearing a century old. Her back legs buckle. It is difficult to stand in one place. Her anus balloons red, her teeth have whittled to brown nubs, and the fur in the crevices of her limbs stinks like cheese.

After the couple retreats to their offices, Gelsomina stands in the center of the first floor and scans the perimeter for potential partners. It is a quiet morning on the street. There are few cars. It is Sunday, and the construction of neighboring homes has ceased for the weekend. Animals creep comfortably onto the property. A lizard suns on a rock in the garden. A raccoon rests at the very top of an adjacent tree.

With the guidance of instinct, Gelsomina begins her endeavors with a flock of birds measured across a branch. She finds them beautiful – gray with a smattering of teal and lilac along their necks, delicate feathers spreading like hands, their synchronized landings. Today, there are sixteen. It is remarkable how small their heads are and their even smaller beaks.

It is not sex she is looking for, but a connection to the external world and its unwritten rules. She has never formed a relationship that does not consist of lopsided intimacies or competition. Standing on the edge of a floral living room rug, Gelsomina switches her nub of a tail to the side. The audience of birds nuzzle one another as they wait for her act to begin. She bows to the birds, then rolls onto her back in submission. From her splayed position, she turns her neck to look up at the flock. Most remain curious though a few have taken flight with her sudden movements.

Gelsomina rests on the ground reflecting on who she is pretending to be. For a few seconds, she wishes to sleep on the cool tile instead of going through with this courtship. Then, in a stubborn fit, she pushes herself up and stands to pee. The remaining birds fly away, two by two, until she is alone within her own expanding puddle.

She attempts the same ritual with the raccoon, a snake curled in the bushes, and a lost house cat patiently waiting to be found on the front doormat. It is a choreography of advances, a confused burlesque with no intention for cohesion, for cohabitation, nor for commitment. The responses to her advances are of fear. Gelsomina is an unknown entity, one associated with the dangers of a manmade structure. She is convinced it is much too late. For her there is no one, nothing.

Wendy comes downstairs to pools of urine littered across the open room. She cleans Gelsomina's spreading messes in gloves with blue paper towels, then removes her water bowl from the floor. Wendy holds Gelsomina in her arms, examining her face as she scrubs her body in the sink. A warm towel is removed from the dryer and wrapped around Gelsomina. Wendy fluffs her in quick motions.

The amount of urine soaking the paper towels appears disproportionate to Gelsomina's frame, Wendy thinks, and is more like the production of a big dog. Wendy feels that it is wrong to ration Gelsomina's water when one of the medications prescribed to her makes her thirsty. Wendy feeds her a CBD gummy for anxiety, which makes Gelsomina drowsy and distorts her vision, in hopes that she will get some rest.

As she drifts to sleep, Gelsomina succumbs to the futility of her last-ditch efforts to embolden herself, and live fully, rather than within the boundaries of habit. There is no use in trying. She sinks back into the comfort of the familiar. The worms are a nuisance again, rather than a guide. In the suspension of a dream, she thinks of ways to rid herself of the parasites. Before giving in to sleep, her only remaining option is to end her life and reincarnate as a worm.

Gelsomina wakes up alone on the couch. In a fit of anxiety, she takes the plush ball to a corner of the house to lick its matted skin. The woman has driven off somewhere and the man has wandered outside with Zampanò. She stuffs half the ball in her mouth and sucks it sopping wet. She debates ripping it open. The thing has a horrid stench and is nearing the end of its use. It would be smart to dissect the ball and remove the squeaking creature now before the woman throws it away and replaces it as she has done many times before. But Gelsomina is exhausted and the thought of tearing open the ball is so out of the question that she stops licking it altogether.

Racing through her mind is the concept of a long life with one being instead of two, the couple. Her pair might be out there, enacting a ghostly duet without her. Her inability to find her pair must have to do with her small stature, timidity, and confinement. No matter – there would have been things expected of her as one half of a pair, such as the consideration of another, giving over her body, and growing many small versions of herself. The fetus is a parasite.

Clinking at the back of her mind is a fair-weather notion about autonomy. Gelsomina enjoys sitting and looking out the window at the water and trees, all their fluid motions. It is the only thing left that Gelsomina wants to do. She leaves behind the plush ball and slinks beneath the wooden console. The privacy and darkness of the space soothe her to sleep.

When Gelsomina wakes again, both the man and the woman are asking her to be near them, to crawl out and join them in the light of day. They are on their knees with their chins grazing the floor. She can only see the lengths of their peering faces. The man places his finger on her front paw. Without hesitating, Gelsomina licks it repeatedly, as though his ribbed nail were the plush ball. He tastes of salt. Zampanò forces himself between the couple but cannot fit his barrel-sized chest beneath the wooden console. She growls at the sight of his flaring snout until the couple shoos him away. He stands at a distance to watch. They continue with their song, a repetitive oration about *good Gelsomina*, along with the promise of a treat.

She would not mind a treat. Lately, the couple has been giving her a sticky substance in the shape of a square that tastes of liver. They place one next to her paw, which she eats. The jelly gets stuck between her teeth. The woman holds out another treat, shaking it back and forth in her hand as though its movement will further coerce Gelsomina out of her cave. Gelsomina smells a scent like soil on the breath and anuses of the couple. The taste of the treat lingers in her mouth. Eventually she slides out from under the console, if only to not feel so trapped.

Metaplasm

All stories traffic in tropes, i.e., figures of speech necessary to say anything at all. Trope (Greek: *tropós*) means swerving or tripping. All language swerves and trips; there is never direct meaning; only the dogmatic think that trope-free communication is our province. My favorite trope for dog tales is 'metaplasm'. Metaplasm means a change in a word, for example by adding, omitting, inverting, or transposing its letters, syllables, or sounds. The term is from the Greek *metaplasmos*, meaning remodeling or remolding. Metaplasm is a generic term for almost any kind of alteration in a word, intentional or unintentional. I use metaplasm to mean the remodeling of dog and human flesh, remolding the codes of life, in the history of companion-species relating... Metaplasm can signify a mistake, a stumbling, a troping that makes a fleshly difference. For example, a substitution in a string of bases in a nucleic acid can be a metaplasm, changing the meaning of a gene and altering the course of a life. Or, a remolded practice among dog breeders, such as doing more outcrosses and fewer close line breedings, could result from changed meanings of a word like 'population' or 'diversity'. Inverting meanings; transposing the body of communication; remolding, remodeling; swervings that tell the truth...

Donna Haraway, *The Companion Species Manifesto*

Immutable Was the Field Alone

Why have I been put here to listen? Silence might not be anywhere. What I can and cannot hear. Or have chosen not to hear. Low frequency of a constant, pulsing note. Gentle humming arriving beneath the stones. The water, too, bubbling in stride. Inhibited voices mingling with old thoughts, so stale and gone. Railing through like a bird cutting air. Fluttering up thick space. Every word has been heard. Every skimpy article of expression directed at me or not. The man and the woman's voices accumulating like gunk between two hard surfaces. Binding my solitary edges. A spongy and sustained chatter. Nothing can be muted. As if I were made to endure it all. Noises erupting in layers, in waves above a grumbling static. Rhythmic buzzing that if I think about too hard, I vomit. The man, the woman, the stone, the water. Hearing for an outcome. For the determination of my next predetermined move. Biding one's time. Passing into sleep, yet the panic remains. A tittering leaf on a bluff. The only antidote is my form against another form. Conjoining to a limb, stripping it of warmth. The house hog grinds into a rubber cylinder. He snores on a rug by the front door. I do not know where. Sometimes in a corner where two of the same walls meet. Examining the surface, and the sustained interaction having found stillness. Wondering if the words are lodged in the angle. The unknown enlarging the known. My own real heart bumping into me. Abdominal heat lowers, stimulating an eruption of my erotic pulse. Anxious pitter-patter and there I am in a fit of uncertainty pounding myself against the back of my plush ball. Admittedly a large focus. One that is rotund and challenging to mount. Wriggling from here to there. A contrary object made to move. Yet soft against my navel. A willing object so kind to me. Stripped of personal expression, itself a blank page. This movement was once the release of concern. The terror discharging in rapid motions. Now a new feeling in the same region. A wanton feeling. But there is still something missing, never reached. A climb without descent. Ongoing symphony of genital cohesion. Petering out. Nothing. I think if more is in the distance. If I stop too short. Regardless, the repetitive action has never been rewarded. Chastised by the man and the woman for what could be so wrong. I know for certain it is a common effort. I have been mounted once or twice before by the house hog. Facsimile of what is meant to happen. I was lying on my stomach. Bestride by the swine, my lower back feeling the weight of him. No recourse. Only commotion from the man and the woman. Saddled with his misguided senses, lost in that eruption of low-riding feelings. It has nothing to do with me, just as the plush ball is not my keystone. No nucleus of affection. It is the act itself. The house hog has minute rushes of desire unlike mine, drawn out. Today I have put aside my plush ball in search of the real. Where could that be? Beyond, in a space like a sliver. But also, here is a rectangle of land. A hybrid of the real and the made-up. An existing situation, demarcated and littered with steel chairs. Yellow pollen-stained objects wet in dew. I wind beneath their forms with a brighter sense of surroundings. Early morning, sunny in a way that makes it blue. Of course, these are only details of the ground and near-ground. Disturbed soil and dead worms in shriveled spirals. Then, scattered, and violent hues of lime dusted across. Stripped bark confined around plants sitting belly up, revealing all of themselves. More bashful hedges wrapped in a coat of green. Who knows what goes on in the trees. Honest in their presentation. All their matter on display yet I will never see that high. Well, the light is amorphous today. And here I am hoping to find what is actual within the boundaries. Cruel container, graceless tormentor. It is a thing that I cannot think about too intensely. Another example of the mind pushed into a narrow ravine. One, two, one and two. Careful steps lead me in my same worn-down paths. Circles of an ancestry that includes only me. Past other me and I before that. They could be walking here when I am not here. One step, two, and one other and one other into patchy understandings. What is happening within me is not so different. The twain creatures' refusal to mate makes my interior seem dry and flat. That river of health receded, revealing a cracked bed. Hard earth breaking into shards. The mucus accumulating on each creature, so thick it solidifies. Struggling to slide. No spit swapping, form coddling. Dehydration, repulsion of liquid in unfertilized ground. Something I never noticed in myself until life has worked to live inside. Not empty, though quite barren. It is hard not to wonder what made me this way. If it might be caused by the limitations of an organized world. Spatial illusion of control. Once again, there is nothing but to take the next step along my loop. Shaky joints thrust forward in a revolution of searching. I ignore the weight of webbed trees growing out of sand. Around their central vein rings of bygone water. Here is where I will try to find attachment regardless of my arid nature. Making myself available via scent. Envisioning a willingness of all the orifices. Specifically, to bind myself to a shade of cinnamon, the ochre calling of between-bushes. To discover myself within, to lodge coconspiratorially and remain in the uncultivated, the luxuriant growth of thick. Up the chest a stretch of white. Only the legs of the fox are the same color as mine, black. Behind, a feathered tail the girth of my middle. As a distraction in my trotting, sniffing, and dreaming. I am stopped in my tracks: does this animal know what it is like to produce more animals? As in, whether it is concerned with the reproduction when it is already a production, *a being.* For all I know it could already be holding life below the chest. Drinking so another can drink, eating so another can eat. Is this meant to be a good feeling? Internal growth of another. Or is it timid like me? Quick to leave like me? Uncertainty in every action. Hesitancy in every step. Barks and yelps arriving only sparingly. Faltering halfway and rising in pitch. Oh, but this animal must be stronger than me. Willing to move in directions of self-determination. Rightfully so, this animal is my sole decision. Righteous focus. The one reason. Pit of mercy. Every step forward is bloated with the possibility of the fire red. But all that seems to endure within this boundary is the animals' floral scent, and right beneath, sulfur. Awful in a way I like. The worms' desire for life seeps into me. Pressing the soft spot between my eyes, I am feral. Imprint on the brain, a damaging sort of touch that has left me changed for good. The change? My awareness of a well, not within me but beside me, in front of, or even behind me.

Void of orange and of love. That soft whine in the distance. One of forty different sounds I have counted from the creature. Where I could be. Investigation of the animal's underground den. As if I would be wanted there. As if I am wanted anywhere. Touch is offered to me as a question. Death specter. In some ways I am already gone. Me. Ideas of want and need shed. I once was who I never was once again. And the parts of me that are here, they are warm spots in a sea of cold. Squib of existence. Backward currents attempting to overcome the big sea. Look – I am only here to suck on plush balls. I hold all their parts tightly beneath my mouth in the cavity of my sternum. A hoarder of the insignificant because there is nothing else for me to have. To hold. I am the one who is had. I cannot have. It must be more than my size. As if my devil may care. Few things I am trusted with. Not even my food, the release of my bowels. What I smell. Empty-handed, here I am, having given up on the orange creature, crouching on a square of artificial ground straining to relieve myself. I watch a placid lake as stiff and rigid as me. My form asks for alleviation, wrenching for the release. Curling beneath myself, begging. Opening and closing, opening again, releasing only air. I toddle forward. Embarrassment of my inability. I search for the last time I was able to do so. My mind is useless. Three acorn shells tossed from the top of a tree, landing in front of my squat. A creature's nest. Mockery of absent stools. One more acorn tipping over, bounces. Running down a trunk, the creature finds another of its kind. And who determines where they can go on the land? Why have we not interacted? These are the questions that expand and pop consecutively. Another attempt, holding my breath and pushing. Oh, there they are in a sex chase. Procreation blues. Up and down the bark, and here I am alone and impotent. In my gut, a bed of stones. A prayer for fluidity, which I have come to believe is a secret string of emotion that is felt synchronously by the real. To have freedom within. Ability to conduct the way I wish to be conducive. Perhaps this is the worms' way of refusing to leave. Perhaps they are shutting me down. Hard to know whether to prepare for an end. Imminent and pressing into me from all sides. But also, out from within. It has been a day of misses and I am a field of simple grasses. An organism that others wind between, making sense of me. Hitched to dirt. Blown around and meant to be like that. I do not think I have weight in the way that matters. Tethered to the purpose of another. There is something, straining, attempting, nothing. I give up twice more and leave the spot where I am told to relieve myself, one direction in many that strictly enforce how I live. I think back to when I have ever been a blank slate. If there was a time when I moved and considered without barrier. A field of simple grasses. The voice of the man and the woman in my head, and also the stone, the water, the trees, the land, and the presence of my false animals cleared of their false hearts: *no, no, no, no, no, no, no, no, no, no, no, no, no, no, no, no, no, no, no, no, no, no, no, no, no, no, no, no, no, no, no, no, no, no, no, no, no, no, no, no.*

Little in Many Places

Gelsomina teeters over to the edge of the living room, bracing as the worms induce sharp contractions within her. The couple is on the couch with Zampanò nestled between them. His snoring hums in and out. Gelsomina lies down on the floor as the couple calls for her. Their summons are criticisms. Footsteps arrive and Gelsomina stiffens in anticipation of being lifted. Instead, the plush ball is placed beside her paw and, in its untouched state, is ripe with disapproval.

The smell of blood sausages wafts throughout the first floor. Forks and knives scrape plates. She licks open the wound in her paw. Wendy says *stop*. Gelsomina hovers her chin above the paw, then licks it once more. It crosses her mind that she does not know what happened before this moment. There is the window. The house is one big window. Silverware is set down on a plate, and the plate on the glass table with a clang. A wholly teal bird and a wholly lilac bird flash in front of her. She thinks about love, but it does not matter. She thinks about leaving, but where would she go?

Gelsomina cannot grasp nonexistence. It is a place that is nowhere and therefore should not be feared. It is nothing, like the belly of the steel grate. The idea reels without closure. If she did not exist, the *there* where she would go would not really be *there*. And who says she would go where there is no *there* to go?

Lodged between the lake and sky is the gray horizon line wavering in her half-wakened state. She envisions that one day she will end up as one piece of its length, bending and contracting within an ambiguous whole. It looks far but right. Sometimes her mind drifts to this point in space and weightlessness floats within her. All her ailments melt away. There is a feeling that is the absence of feeling. A place that is nowhere and therefore has no feeling. A place that is nowhere and therefore has no feeling and no one should have feelings about. Gelsomina suspects that her present life must come to a stop. Her senses are failing. Touch poorly mediates surroundings. Sometimes she is only a physical form. Other times, she is only a mind.

The worms gurgle within her. It might be the drugs disturbing them. She was fed three pieces of turkey earlier in the day but cannot determine the quantity of pills concealed within them. Gelsomina feels herself getting smaller. Her joints hurt within her endlessly shrinking frame. She trusts that the woman has fed her a substance that she needs. Not that this is without effect. Gelsomina regularly comes to in a corner of the house with her back legs tucked beneath her. The light of a day passes by in a blink. Doubt creeps in.

To be sedated; to be split in two. Gelsomina is certain that she is being divided by the worms. Eventually she will become invisible to the naked eye. So, too, will the worms. Together or not, they will morph into new forms. Breaking, congealing, splintering. Are the worms bound to her? Are they bound to each other? Was she once bound to her lost pair, the one whom she never found?

She considers whether her selves can divide honestly. Meaning, whether the selves that make up a being can individualize. A worm cut in two. A worm cut in thirds growing new hearts. A mass shedding from their mouths, making new orbs. In other words, she wonders whether the many parts of her, with their different motives and feelings, can live on their own. Maybe she can exist in many places. At some point, Gelsomina's suffering must cease, for things so small should not feel so much pain.

Rising from her place by the window, she walks over to the glass bridge within the house. The design choice, if it were to appear in one's dreams, symbolizes a difficult transition in life that requires courage. It might also represent what one is unwilling to confront. The glass bridge is a place that Gelsomina quickly trots across in fear of falling to her death. It is about ten times her length and spans a pond. Today a small bird flies a figure eight.

The couple is immune to the effects of the bridge. Countless times they have stopped on its surface. This is no surprise. There are many rules that do not apply to the couple. They are not affected by the shock of the Invisible Force and move freely away from the property. Their food is not rationed. They are allowed upstairs.

Gelsomina stands at the edge of the glass bridge and examines the pond below. Zampanò is sleeping on the lap of the man. The couple watches television without having noticed her. In this blip of autonomy, Gelsomina does not allow pause. She expects the fall to be quick. One paw catches the surface, then the next, until she stands, trembling, at the center of the bridge. Surprised by her survival, Gelsomina sits down on the glass. She watches the movements of organisms below. A lizard crawls across wet soil. The bird finishes, satisfied with its exploration, and leaves the open-air room.

John turns to watch. He speaks to Wendy about Gelsomina's mental state, saying that she is no longer herself and, pointing to Gelsomina on the glass bridge, 'Jesus – have you ever seen Gelsomina stop on the glass?' The couple watches her, and their attention wakes Zampanò, who glances over at Gelsomina before placing his head back down.

Gelsomina lies on the bridge and imagines a black hole. The worms are with her, too, stuck in limbo. They comment that though there are walls, it is so dark that they could be anywhere. Gelsomina wishes to fold into herself. Otherwise, there seems to be no way out of them. Or for them, no way out of her.

Her despair is not entirely due to her failed romances. She is unwanted, but Gelsomina also concludes that her chances to experience life beyond the glass house are dwindling. Perhaps the suitors she solicited did not respond because they sensed that they are tools to understand the worms, or herself.

Gelsomina sits up on her hind legs in pain. There is a shift in her guts. She is merely a willing vessel. Relief comes when one worm wraps around the other. The worms' heads stack and the day breaks open. When the worms are not fighting, they are a good weight, like pressure on a wound. Gelsomina sways with them; she dances. Her smooth belly grazes the glass surface. Her burdened hips make waves. Outside, the fox is caught in a steel trap. Today's sun shower is a symbol of a funeral. The grass is green, and the sky is blue.

After finding more of Gelsomina's mess in the house, Wendy picks her up from the glass bridge and carries her over to where she courted the birds. She points at Gelsomina's drying urine, has her smell it, and repeats that she is *very bad*. As Gelsomina walks away, she hears Wendy spraying liquid from a bottle and turns to watch her on hands and knees, rubbing blue paper towels in wide circles.

Gelsomina is reminded of her full bladder and walks into the kitchen to urinate once more. Afterward, she wades through the puddle to a low shelf where she finds a half-eaten bag of pork rinds poorly enclosed by a metal clip, which clicks off when Gelsomina knocks the bag onto the floor. Before she can get her few decent teeth around a rind, Zampanò barges in to devour the remainder of the bag. He sniffs her urine and leaves. Gelsomina follows him around the perimeter of the house.

Finding the new puddle, Wendy nudges Gelsomina out onto the porch and tells her the sun will do her good. Gelsomina lays on the stone patio like a sphinx, missing the glass barriers of the house that tell her who she is supposed to be. Outside, she forgets. Her thoughts stop momentarily, then altogether. Vertigo washes between her ears. She observes the rectangular plot of land. Once Gelsomina feels that she has properly lain in the sun, she rises from her place and wanders as though she is being led somewhere.

Gelsomina lingers in the line of the Invisible Force, expecting to be electrocuted. She assumes the shock will catch her off guard, evacuating her from her form. Gelsomina worries that the Invisible Force has been removed, or that she has been moving in circles. She considers leaving. Instead, she finds a familiar spot by a dogwood bush where she was shocked once before and waits.

Animal Suicide

> Beginning to think is beginning to be undermined.
> Society has but little connection with such beginnings.
> The worm is in man's heart. That is where it must be
> sought. One must follow and understand this fatal game
> that leads from lucidity in the face of existence to flight
> from light.
>
> Albert Camus, 'Absurdity and Suicide',
from The Myth of Sisyphus

It is not proven that animals knowingly kill themselves, though there are numerous recorded incidences of depression, self-harm, and heroic displays in which animals have taken their own lives. Émile Durkheim published his study *Suicide* in 1897, which articulates their various methods of self-destruction, including animal victims who may or may not have understood the outcome of their choices. Durkheim argues that animals know what they are doing. His study was produced during a time when the popular thought was that animals would commit a noble act of self-destruction due to human mistreatment, though they were unaware of the permanence of their actions.

A broad discussion of animal suicide was spurred by the scorpion who, when surrounded by a ring of flames without any method of escape, chose to poison itself with its own tail. In 1845, a Newfoundland dog was reported to have repeatedly thrown itself into the water and, after being rescued a few times, gone out once more and held its head under ocean waves until it died. A duck, after the death of its mate, is reported to have drowned itself, too. In the 1970s, the retired dolphin performer Kathy, who had been held captive and alone at the Miami Seaquarium, sank to the bottom of a concrete tank and never resurfaced. Others have noted this act of will over the last few centuries, stating that dogs will commonly starve themselves following the death of their guardians, dragging their emaciated bodies to their humans' graves. Bees, wasps, and ants have offered their own lives to protect their colonies from attackers.

This choice might not always be the whim of the animal, but rather the organisms who occupy their bodies. Take the case of some parasites who control their host's cognitive function for their own benefit. Parasites have been reported to convince insects and other terrestrial hosts to drown themselves, enabling the parasite to enter an aquatic environment for its own reproduction. Other parasites have convinced their hosts to approach their predators so that they will be killed. While infiltrating the neurochemical pathways of a rat's brain, *Toxoplasma* has not only erased its fear of cats, but has made the smell of the predator's urine arousing. Rats are coaxed in by the scent and eaten, allowing the parasite to enter the tissues of the feline, its preferred host.

Humans are also cognitively affected by parasites, with one-third of people on earth carrying around the organisms in their brains. E. Fuller Torrey, a psychiatrist working at the Stanley Medical Research Institute, found that people with high levels of the *Toxoplasma* parasite are more likely to give birth to a child who will later become schizophrenic. A later study in Denmark found that infected women were 54 percent more likely to attempt to take their own lives, a finding that was true even of those without a history of mental illness. The parasite will make its host more insecure, guilty, and depressed. The link between the parasite and suicide is not always straightforward. With the presence of a parasite, the immune system produces high levels of cytokines, which has been connected to suicide attempt. Scientists are left with the conundrum – are the suicides caused by the parasite, or by the bodily response to the parasite?

~

Entwined in a loop of instinct, lapping and overlapping, my pair and I once again become one. The scarcity of knowing, the abundance of resources – a disorienting reality that requires that we, for at least a moment, attach as we were when born. A deep emotion is funneling through the being. Our surroundings tighten in a way that feels close to death. A steady hum loses pitch and pace. Bound, our measured purrs lull us into compatibility. We are a series of vermilion margins extending into vermilion margins. One of my ends is held beneath the center of my pair, and one of its ends beneath mine, a provisional shelter. The taste of my pair and the being mix sour. The wave passes. Just as before, my pair relinquishes itself from the assemblage of our making. Undone in the vacuum, a shallow cool slips in. I have been wrenched like an umbilical cord.

We return to an existence adjacent to each other. I am overtaken by a transient confusion. From the beginning, my pair has fastened me here like a linchpin. I am ashamed that I doubt myself and that I rely on our attachment. There is one resilient part of me that asks: is it only the idea of the orb that stirs me? Perhaps my pair is right in that I will be unsatisfied anywhere I go. Then, I remember our early days, how we were coddled by the slow-moving and bright.

There is something I am doing that my pair does not like. I can tell by its recoil but cannot decipher the problem with my behavior. My pair is repulsed by me. As a gesture of goodwill, I dive headfirst into an interior wall of the organism and attach myself for as long as I can stand not moving. *We are new*, I remind myself while fused to the wall and think to tell my pair as much. *We are new at life and have had the wrong frame of reference.*

With my head buried, all the vibrations recede. It is like endlessly falling into a pit. Mentally I am erased. As time passes in this position, I encounter new voices, the memories of other worms, dull and just out of reach. They speak of the stone, elixir of life, the site of immortality. I imagine my underbelly on a hard, hot surface. We digest the stone. We turn the world over. We participate in the formation of the stone and its monuments. For the first time it occurs to me that this being might have other organisms harbored within it, too, those who have died and fossilized in its making.

I remove my head with the firm decision that I will no longer remain in this being. I will not hatch and stay as so many others have surely hatched and stayed. Breaking our silence, I explain to my pair that only in my dreams do I find relief. I tell my pair that if it refuses to leave with me, I will sing. I will continue to rap my head before the dead and enact violent noise. And then, in the sudden relief of quietude, my pair will realize that I am gone.

At the time, I was not looking for an exit. Moving around, as I always do after I feel that I have been still for too long, a part of the damp wall lifted. I was too shocked to push it further. I told my pair, and it said I was simply imagining a way out. It said my desires fabricated an opportunity to leave. Then my pair told me to forget that flap. I was caught between two modes. One part of me was guided by the overwhelming need to find a new way of being, while the other felt harnessed to my pair. Uncertainty above all else has prevented my departure.

My plan is to push against the flap and set on a path to be released. Recognizing my resolve, my pair says, *What if it is worse on the other side? What if we are not safe?* I am surprised my pair considers us *we*, a pair. My pair keeps a safe distance between us. I said to myself, *I must not grasp who I am or how I act. I must be twisted.* My pair tells me to get on with it already. *If you are going to leave*, my pair says, *go ahead and leave.* The statement catches me by surprise. Beneath the frustration of my pair, I sense pleasure. For the first time, I realize that my pair might want me gone.

How will I exist on my own? And what if we are here to be born again? What if my pair is right, and we are not in a large space but a small one? In other words, what if we are wrapped in the casing of a dark orb within the casing of an endless expansion of orbs? In this scenario, there would be no flap, no road leading elsewhere, and I will experience an infinite hatching.

One reason why my pair is not interested in the flap is because it leads south, whereas my pair wants to move north. My pair tries to convince me that it is drier in the northern parts of the organism, but I do not trust this. Rather than debate the topography, I mention ({i}) again. My pair shuts down, ignoring me, but there is nothing else for it to do but listen. If I refuse to reproduce, it can consume nutrients and wait. My pair does not believe in the act of (((((((((selfing))))))))), claiming it is unnatural. I explain that ({i}) is fading from us, because we are living incorrectly, occupying the form of an organism that is dying. My pair shakes one end of itself in anger, then takes off.

After a few days of speaking about the flap, to placate me, my pair says to imagine we are in moist soil. The others are there, too, the three who died, and we are wrapped in secret, all distinctly alive. The bright orb above illuminates our little one. I try to imagine this, but it does not help. I have never sung before, and it comes out at first in moans. It feels good and deep, and I echo.

In fear, my pair curls into a spiral. I sing louder, and my pair tightens into its own center. As I sing, my pair hums nondescript vibrations to soothe itself. I describe in song the maze of ({i}) in beautiful, intricate detail. The whorl of my pair's ridged tube trembles, while the length of me fills with a collage of all the sounds I heard while inside the orb – the water, the wind, the rain, the grunting, the squealing, the laughing, the dying – reverberating against the fabric of the universe.

Later I realized that I had begun the process for (((((((((selfing))))))))). An orb forms at the threshold of one of my vermilion margins. I wonder if this orb of worms will also be me, if my pair will finally be happy with all these new versions of me. Over time, the budding orb enlarges. In awe of its stubborn path to independence, I am quiet about this new orb. My pair, who refuses to touch me, is unaware of the growth at my collar. I am slow and still in anticipation of its gentle break from my form, until ((((((((((*Oh!*)))))))))).

( ) Form

A form is a type of something; to make exist; existence; to be. It can be a set of organisms; the nest of a hare; a long, thin seat without a back; how something is done; a room where students go for their teachers to record them as present; mathematical expression; linguistic expression; artistic expression; literary expression; poetical expression; to arrange or give shape; a contour making a thing visible and measurable; a thing that is tangible; to be free; to have life; to fix; the manifestations of a word. It is to be filled out and turned in, usually printed, or typed in black ink on white paper with blank spaces for information.

Form comes from the Latin *forma*, a feminine noun meaning mold, form, and beauty. It is used in common phrases such as: to be at the top of one's form; poor form; in no way, shape, or form. Form is hardheaded and willing, static and amorphous, obscure and clear, organic and synthetic, active and reactive. It holds and excludes, crushes and expands, births and terminates. One can never truly understand a form, an entity so broad that it transcends meaning. Literal definitions are a reduction of form. The absurd or surreal might more readily capture the form being described. Attempting to box in a form will only push it further away.

There are rhetorical forms employed by writers to evoke emotion in readers: expository, narrative, persuasive, comparative, descriptive, simile, metaphor, hyperbole, alliteration, satire, connotation, cause and effect, problem and solution, paradox, climax, ethos, pathos, logos, kairos, epithet, meiosis, personification, parallelism, and synecdoche. These tactics are used to gain the reader's trust, so that they will accept and adopt the writer's point. They are used to braid texture into a text, clarify a message, nudge in specific directions, and occasionally deflect from the realities, information, or truths that a writer cannot know, illustrating the familiar phrase – *form of distraction*.

The primary elements of architecture are two supposed opposites: form and space. They allow for three-dimensionality and are visible with light and shadow. Form applies to both the interior and exterior structures. In 27 BC, Vitruvius named the three elements of architecture as strength (stability), use (function), and form (beauty); solid, useful, and beautiful. The form of a building comprises shapes, lines, masses, volumes, geometries, scales, and materials. It is perceptible, divides space, is additive or subtractive, and has rhythm. For two centuries, it has been said that form follows function. The functions of a space and its users should give way to form. Architects are finding form – the material object, the structural object.

Form determines the function of beings, and function over time determines their form. Behavior and emotion are derivatives of form, and the inter- and intra-action of forms. A being or thing can transform, undergoing a dramatic change, such as when the heat from the eruption of Mount Vesuvius turned a man's brain to glass. His remains were found in a wooden bed; the only known person to undergo vitrification. *Formulation* is the act of creation; a material made from a formula. A *formula* is a principle, a set of words, a recipe, a collection of symbols, or convention. *Isomorphic* means to have the same form; *iso* meaning identical, and *morph* meaning form or shape. *Morph* is a spinoff of metamorphosis.

A *life form* is nominally self-explanatory, although its meaning is murky. *Life* is living, a concept that means to be alive. The meaning of *alive* is *not dead*, also animated, responsive, in existence or use. The delineation is muddied by a third state one occupies between life and death. After a being dies, their cells survive and take on new forms. A system of electrical circuits keeps the cells alive. Scientists revived a pig brain by pumping drugs into the organ four hours after the pig's death, though the animal was not considered alive itself. The findings draw into question what forms belong to whom, if smaller forms belong to the larger forms that host them, and vice versa.

Delineations among forms of thought are arbitrary. Philosophical and aesthetic phenomena have always played a role in science, from the illustration of theories to the aiding of new revelations. Friedrich August Kekulé dreamt of a snake biting its own tail, allowing him to unlock the ringed structure of benzene, one that symbolizes infinity in its cyclic nature. Niels Bohr articulated the structure of the atom after a dream about the solar system. Both image and language, sensical and nonsensical, are swapped and lent out.

*

The form of the immaterial is that of the incorporeal: the spiritual ether, hidden truths, memory, cosmic matter, or anything that does not consist of matter, as in that which has an imperceptible physicality. The immateriality of the immaterial is continuously disputed, prodded by questions such as: Do all forms have matter? Do thoughts have form? Are thoughts matter? How much does a thought weigh? Is it tangible? When depicted, formless matter is illuminated and effervescent, a sphere with countless intersecting lines emerging from its form and extending outward.

These concepts are better left undefined rather than specifically misunderstood. Formless intermediaries are continuously undermined in their classification as non-forms. Consciousness, for example, is ephemeral, difficult to pin down in origin and reach, its meaning stunted to an act of awareness and perception. Yet its architecture is found in the form of long, slender, cylindrical microtubules inside brain neurons. The warm quantum vibrations within the vermiform play a part in the orchestration of consciousness.

The corporeal form is defined in opposition to a soul. Synonyms of *corporeal* are *material, substantive, phenomenal, anatomical, fleshly, objective, sensible, tangible, carnal,* and *animal*. Antonyms of *corporeal* include *spiritual, mental, cerebral, intellectual, non-physical, immaterial, ethereal,* and *bodiless*. Legally, the corporeal includes the animate and the inanimate, encompassing anything that is tangible, such as land that is *immovable corporeal* and money that is *movable corporeal*. Both are deemed by many people to be more valuable than simply *corporeal*.

Continuity is misconstrued as the antithesis of form; that form is a byproduct of distinctions and delineations. The *transcorporeal* amends a common misconception that a corporeal form is not porous and operates as a boundary between the internal and the external. Rather, the corporeal is highly penetrable, allowing what is out to come in. Everything and everybody are intermeshed, inseparable from all environments and surroundings. For instance, the larva of a parasitic worm arrives through a bare foot walking in soil, and stays in that form, making a home of it, and causing the form to itch, wheeze, lose its appetite, and drop in weight.

It is this last understanding of form that sits at the edges of ({i}). An arbitrary thing that serves as a permeable and deficient demarcation between i and its distinct involvement with cosmic matter, space, time, and other forms, (). It is legible in its thinness and the way it loosely takes on the shape of cosmic matter. It is a shawl to the more substantial parts of ({i}). *Skin* is not what is being described. This form is the boundary of the space that is taken up in the world. It includes the energy of the being, along with its superficialities.

Few will acknowledge the true state of their i, nor the cosmic matter that binds them together as one entity. They are very acutely only aware of (). And () is only ever I, a version of a self that masquerades as i, but is a farce. I is a thing that is conjured up only in relation to others. I is a divider. It can never be additive and never connect. I will never be separate from (). Whereas i is solitary, a reflection only of the true self. Detached from its frame ({}), i can connect to other naked i's. Altogether, the naked i's become the gelatinous material of the entire universe, the orb.

Salten Hag

I look around to find what annihilated the will to live. The pre-enactment of my end. A torment of imminence. I have been given no reason here other than the strict renunciation decided for me. I rely on the efficacy of prayer in the form of radical discipline, in silence, rationing, and limited movement. I did not feel this way before. What I thought is good is not good on this plane of existence. As if I were beyond all change and alteration. With celibacy I have gone to waste. My semisacred character. Now the impetus to spread myself thin. To evaluate a thing opening wide. Or am I just tired of contemplation? An awakening that I have quickly grown old. Revelation taps on all corners. The sacred word – *No* – rendering false devotion. Oral memorization that never belonged to me. A sentence of coercion. A forest of reason. A desert of monasticism. What would happen if I were to sleep? I have tried to give in and have been told to go on. Demonic forces have entered me. Believe it or not, up to one. The infallible question of many natures. I will never be a unified form, nor eternally valid. I have taken residence here to offer a daily recollection of expiry. A downright march into the uncontained. I examine the things I have denied. Apparently, I cannot go on this way, as I am, defiled by others. Yet I must accommodate the full extent of life. I carry forth. Why has so much time passed until things are asked of me? I wonder if my younger form could handle the weight of other structures. Now I am a salten hag with no outlook but the windowpane. I am a dead sea. The will to live is the will to stand. Bed warmed, here I am. Never have I been more careless. Biding my time though long overdue. Wiped away are the remnants of me. What discipline prescribed but clenching? Preventing relief in all its forms? Continuation for the sake of continuation. What end is the end I deserve to die at the end? The life I could never live. To make higher sense out of anything. To believe in my existence is not the same as to believe in the belief of my existence. I am not omnibenevolent nor merciful. Coming from the inside to define me. Obedience of no clear order. The process of utterance in a disquieting reality. Nothing has been disclosed. I want to know the froth of others. To be aware of the signs of kind. A douse of knowledge. To not have the doing done to me. To regenerate as a spinning crater. Me, an idea.

Bygone Instincts

Zampanò considers whether it is worth the trouble to leap onto the chaise lounge chair. He leans back onto thick hind legs. One hop, another, he is in the air, landing comfortably on the warm cushion. In the distance, a fisherman arrives in a boat. Zampanò imagines himself as the fisherman. He imagines himself as a fish. His eyes blink, then close. Gelsomina briefly struggles to jump onto the lounge chair beside him. Their breathing falls into a rhythmic hum.

The French bulldogs have returned to their typical complaints. They find it unfair that they are living in a room that rises thirteen feet higher than them, with an upper floor they are not allowed to traverse, and that all the food is prepared on counters they cannot see. While listening to the couple's movements up above, Zampanò cries like a baby. Believing that he hears them at the top of the stairs, he sniffles, then lets in a sharp breath before wailing once more.

The day balloons with boredom. Gelsomina heaves the two worms from one side of the glass house to the other. Zampanò bombs ahead as she pauses to catch her breath before the threshold of the glass bridge. Below, in the pond's brown depths, silverfish the size of thumbs swim in disorderly schools. Slick forms disperse at the sight of her. Mere flecks remain in the water. She wishes to be that fleck, that one, too; to be one of many floating.

She turns around in agony as a bird slams into the glass wall. Zampanò rammed into the back door earlier that morning, thinking it had been left open. One after another, the birds' teal necks bend to the clear surface. She recognizes one suitor from the day before by the heart-shaped birthmark on its chest. Then, flashes of pink feet and black eyes; their regular thuds.

After sniffing forgotten corners, Zampanò circles back at one end of the rectangular house to arrive at Gelsomina's side overlooking the pond. Hundreds of tadpoles have transformed into tiny translucent frogs scattershot across the glass. The French bulldogs admire their pastel-colored organs; the heart that bleeds purple into the throat; and the eggs, like limes, crowding along a single, central vein.

Their transparent forms pulse arrhythmically. Vocal sacs inflate beneath thin lips. The nostrils close and air vibrates against the lungs, letting out a trilling song. Listening to the symphony, the French bulldogs dwell on the appearance of the frogs, and whether they, too, began in water. They think back as far as their minds allow. Gelsomina's first memory is of drowning.

Wendy arrives behind Gelsomina and Zampanò. She is also reminded of beginnings. The creatures rearrange their bulbous toes across the window, suctioning and withdrawing, leaving smudges in their path. Gelsomina shifts her legs under the weight of the worms, then belches. Wendy crouches between the French bulldogs. Gelsomina's belly feels fuller than the day before and

Wendy notes that she must call the veterinarian, patting her softly while lost in the requirements of this pending task. Gelsomina belches once more. Wendy tells the French bulldogs a tale about how frogs were tadpoles that fell from the sky, that they sing during torrential rains to kindle the birth of more tadpoles.

Another Godforsaken Bitch

Nomen est omen. Zampanò is adjacent to Zumpano, or Zupan, the name for a district administrator of the Byzantine Empire; a word meaning chief, leader, or headman. A name influences how one treats another, and how one treats oneself. The naming and gendering of the two animals inevitably sways the behavior of the couple toward their two dogs, affecting how they read and react to the animals, and in turn, how the animals react to them and their attitudes, as well as the behaviors they believe that they can get away with.

The couple waited twelve years to find Zampanò and complete the unit from their favorite Fellini film, *La Strada*, which they saw together at an independent movie theater, just a few days after meeting by chance in a bar. The groups of friends they had separately arrived with gradually collided at a standing table. First, one of the men playfully taunted two of the women. Then another man joined in on the conversation, and the taunt. Finally, over the course of the night, the two groups of four became one.

Wendy was the first to leave. It was late and she was hitching a cab home. John, a little drunk, stumbled out of the bar. He asked if she would grab a cup of coffee with him at a diner around the corner. He would buy her breakfast. It was three in the morning. They shared a plate of buttered toast and scrambled eggs, sausage, and a stack of two hotcakes. He ate more than she did, lapping up his food in a pool of syrup.

By this time, John had sobered up and was more talkative than when he had been drunk.

They discovered that they were both designers. He preferred exterior; she, interior. He asked her many questions regarding her line of work, where she was from, the size of her family, the size of her apartment, the things she liked to do when she was not designing or with her small family from Virginia or sleeping in her studio apartment.

Wendy has always liked movies. At the time, she was particularly drawn to anything by Fellini. She liked the ornate details of the places and costumes, and his rendering of dreams. John called her days later to invite her to see a one-off showing of *La Strada* at the independent movie theater down the street from his office. He will never forget how hard she had cried for the Fool.

In the movie, Zampanò is a strongman and womanizer inspired by the pig castrator from Fellini's childhood town, who impregnated a woman said to have given birth to the devil's child. The protagonist travels around the country as a circus strongman, pulling iron chains from his chest. Years after having found Gelsomina in a pet shop, the couple discovered a breeder for their imagined Zampanò. They believed she was the only breeder who could produce such an animal – a woman so in tune with the heat cycles of her female dogs that she could smell whether they were prepared for puppies, and who inseminated them herself with a long pipette of cold semen. The breeder was recommended by a friend who warned them that not all French bulldogs are the same. No, they needed a French bulldog with the correctly sized ears, positioned at 11 a.m. and 1 p.m., as well as a stout body and bulky head, one that was not as bug-eyed as little Gelsomina.

The breeder's resultant litters were nothing short of renowned award winners. After years on a waiting list, the couple was given an enormous French bulldog who had been slated to win dog shows, like his father, but was much too big to compete. As their friend had advised, his ears struck 11 a.m. and 1 p.m. They were not too big to look like a hare, though not too small to look like a bear cub. He had a wide chest and trunk, and his legs were short and strong. The only strange attribute was his missing tail. Most French bulldogs have a stump, whereas he was born without a tail at all. He tumbled into their lives with the personality of a clown.

People are said to have more evident egotistical tendencies than those of animals for reasons including memory, contemplation, hopes and dreams, the expression of judgment, and projection. Having long distanced themselves from other animals, humans are believed to have more complex cultural structures, too. Yet even plants compete for status in the sun. They sabotage their neighbors and assist others by warning of imminent danger.

With the fate of his name, Zampanò managed to evade the cruelty of Fellini's character. The couple was lucky that, though large, Zampanò has never expressed his ego through dominance and violence, but rather through the possessive nature of an only child. But his chest resembles that of the strongman, its weight propelling him forward as though he might tumble over his two front legs at any step.

The couple finds Zampanò to be softer than Gelsomina, who retreats from their touch now. When they knead a knuckle inside his ear, all the wrinkles on his face collapse in relaxation. Their caresses are his lifeline. As Gelsomina has withdrawn with age, he has reveled in the space that has opened in her absence.

Is Gelsomina reminiscent of her matching character in the film? Perhaps the couple has forgotten how Gelsomina used to be in the early years of her life. Like the waif who was sold by her mother to the brute Zampanò, Gelsomina was simultaneously afraid and in awe of her daily happenings. Wide-eyed and mesmerized, the French bulldog used to follow the couple around the house, studying their movements and getting lost in the repetition of a task or sound. She twirled in a circle when something wonderful appeared in their hands, like food or a toy, then dropped to the floor. The girl, like Gelsomina, is mostly silent.

Sometimes when they look at the French bulldog, they recall the character Gelsomina's round face and eyes and the tattered clothes she dragged around. Another godforsaken woman. The character also sobbed for the Fool, dead in the grass on the side of the road. Later, Gelsomina lay to rest in the snow. Her song tolled across the ocean, and Zampanò lived on.

Will Gelsomina ever experience the same confrontation with life and death? The couple doubts it, though they believe this is a good thing. Their Gelsomina will never be plagued with loss nor cruelty. She will blissfully avoid the worst bestial actions of others. They savor this, for when they look at her, they are reminded of their own beginning, a quiet love that, no matter the friction, perseveres.

*

What kind of a bitch could produce such a robust animal as Zampanò? His mother, Lila, lived with a widowed breeder. She was one of eleven permanent French bulldogs in the house, excluding new litters. Lila was favored by the woman, because she produced nine litters in her lifetime. In turn, the woman made six figures. Lila was a mean bitch and no beauty. Over the years she had grown used to the extreme shifts in her body and behavior and had learned to detach herself from her puppies.

When the time for birth would come, she was taken to the veterinarian, where everything went black for a day. She woke back home with new puppies, usually between two to four of them. Her abdomen ached as they searched for her milk. Sometimes Lila would rise from her deep sleep to find that the puppies had already begun taking from her with the breeder's assistance. The week following their arrival was spent sleeping, bathing in warm water, and nursing. Every day, she was given a total allowance of fifteen minutes outside on a leash to urinate. She could not jump nor play.

Each puppy was held to Lila's face for her to lick the perineum, the space between the genitals and anus. When she refused, the breeder stimulated urination and defecation in the pups, holding their anuses under warm water, then to Lila's face again. When puppies are delivered by cesarean section, the bitch might reject or harm them. To prevent any pain that could be caused by their mother, the breeder watched over the litters and facilitated the steps of nature.

Lila carried Zampanò's litter for sixty-three long days. She ate for nearly all of them, then vomited. She shredded paper to build them a nest. Fifty-six days in she began digging holes to nowhere in the fabric of her bed. Fifty-seven – they took away the neighbor's children, who had previously enjoyed visiting after school each day to check her progress. Fifty-eight – Lila sought a place to rest. Days fifty-nine to sixty-three passed like minutes. The puppies were pulled from her deaf and blind. Every day the puppies were weighed. Within ten days they must double in size. Zampanò, who was marked as a male with a dot of red nail polish on his shoulder, had completed the necessary growth in half the time.

Zampanò's early life with Lila was captured by blurred vision. Three bodies lobbed into him as he navigated darkness. The breeder stood over his mother like she needed something. The puppies' eyes and ears had been left uncleaned. She placed Lila closer to them. Lila kicked her puppies' plump bodies as they sought milk from tender spots. Zampanò was too hungry to stop himself. He suckled on his mother's teat as she trembled with rage. She growled, shook, and kicked. The pain shot down into the line across her abdomen and spread like needles into each of her paws. Nothing could prevent him from eating. He grew larger as the other puppies withered. Without food, they would die or later be debilitated. The breeder grew worried, intervening as necessary, but bottle feeding was not a viable alternative to what their mother could offer. The puppies learned to avoid Zampanò's enormous body, dodging his swinging hips and the collapse of his wide head. Lila grew to hate him.

It was a terrible night, one that materialized in Zampanò's mind as simply a shadow. The litter had been sleeping in the same bed as usual. He thought it was a dream: his mother roosting on his sibling like a hen. Its round body was barely visible beneath her. Lila watched the sliver of Zampanò's foggy sight. She kept his gaze, and his sibling did not whimper. As he drifted back to sleep, Zampanò thought it was another vision that had appeared to him in the night.

In the morning all the siblings shuffled around the limp body until the breeder arrived. She did not see the dead puppy at first. It was early, and she walked past their caged-in spot on the kitchen floor to the coffee maker, pressing its button before pouring herself a glass of water. Leaning against the island, she watched the sun rise behind the bed of dogs. Lila was separated from the puppies, as she had been most mornings, refusing to give them warmth. The breeder improvised, bringing in a floor heater, which the puppies were gathered around. They whimpered and wriggled.

Lila watched the breeder, in anticipation, she assumed, of breakfast. All of them moved except for one. The breeder set down the glass and walked over to the bed. This had happened before, yet it shocked her every time. Rather than touch the puppy, she squeezed the squeaker beside its ear. When it did not move, the breeder used a hand to slowly turn the body over and knew upon touching it that the puppy was dead.

The breeder placed the puppy in the garage, which was cold at that time of year, to be taken to the veterinarian later that day. Then the breeder returned to carry Zampanò out of the kitchen and lock him in another room with his own floor heater and a clock to replicate his mother's beating heart. The breeder was kicking herself, for the thought had drifted through her mind yesterday while watching the puppies, and seeing Zampanò's ample size, that he could roll over and suffocate one of the others.

Caged in the darkness beneath a wooden table and four chairs, Zampanò flattened himself on the tile. His eyes had only begun to open. In the other room he could hear his siblings calling for food and his mother scratching the doorframe. The woman talked aloud to herself about sending Zampanò away.

Looking out over the water from the living room of the glass house, Zampanò focuses on a field of pine trees. Otherwise, he sinks into the same hole inside of himself, a place of iniquity from his first weeks alive, when he was blamed for a horrific thing that he did not do. Rather than fret over the memory of his dead sibling, questioning again whether he is guilty of what he was once accused of doing, Zampanò focuses on Gelsomina's fixation with leaving. He smells ammonic beings growing inside of her and worries about their growth. Zampanò hypothesizes the worst, that the new beings will die within her, and that she will die, too.

But he is most concerned about Gelsomina neglecting the beings. She has the same smell as his mother, that of an old blanket, a worn thing that can smother. Zampanò prepares for the arrival of the beings to manifest their birth. He shreds a plush toy to build them a nest. He collects food scraps that he stores beneath their bed. If given the chance, he will make sure they survive. There is plenty of food and warmth to share, and the danger here is little.

Theory of Everything

John aimlessly collects sticks for firewood when he notices movement in his peripheral vision. Peering between the bushes, he sees hundreds of worms gathered in a patch of soil near the water. They are paired off and, though they are without facial expression, appear to be full of joy. The worms' slithering bodies are beautiful. From a distance, he admires their elegant crawl as they carry pieces of raspberries from one shrub into the next.

Setting down the wood he has gathered, John sits in damp soil just above the lick of the lake to observe the creatures. The more he looks, the more worms he sees. On any other day, John would be frustrated about the proliferation of the worms in his backyard, and their ability in numbers to steal nutrients, stunt plant growth, and kill off a garden. Today, he is struck by the existence of their small universe burrowing in the back of his property.

There are so many lives, he thinks. Perhaps it is the change in season that stirs this wistful feeling. The summer light is turning to that of fall, taking on a golden hue. There is more behind the gesture – at the level of the worms, dirtying the back of his pants, acknowledging that the stain will frustrate Wendy when he goes inside. It gnaws at him, the importance of the encounter, and his inclination to stop and take in the environment. In these moments, John understands that he is rarely in tune with what is happening around him.

The answer comes to him, clarifying why he feels propelled to be near the creatures. The worms remind him of string theory, an idea he has been researching on and off over the last few years, one that suggests reality is made up of an infinite number of vibrating strings.

For John, the worms are a vision of this phenomenon that is much more convincing than the renderings of thin, colorful, glowing strings he has seen online. It delights him that one can view this theory of everything in a way that considers the world as made up of endless worms. And in a way, it is true. He thinks of parasites as an example, with just a stretch of the imagination. Laughing to himself, John thinks about the worm as the origin of life. He tips the edge of his boot into the mucky froth of lake water, and a glob of foam attaches to the leather.

John recalls Judd's statement that science is scientific, and art is superstitious. Architecture supposedly unfolds at the intersection of both. Judd writes that architectural knowledge does not accumulate like scientific knowledge. John turns to watch his wife in the kitchen of the glass structure. He sees the art, the architecture. Superstition is present, so is architectural erasure. The house puts people outside, reminding them that their surroundings are eternally fluctuating.

The principles of the unknown, those measures of imprecision and uncertainty, do not discourage John. There is beauty in the fact that there is always more to be learned, that there are facets of existence that will never be known, that transformation is taking place at every stage of life. As he stands up, satisfied,

Gelsomina arrives at his side. She presses into his calf and glances up at him.

He scratches beneath her pink collar, and asks in a high-pitched tone, 'Are you made of worms?'

                                      oOoOo

~~

It seems that in thinking about a good worm and the correct ways of living, my wish for a third was heard and answered. It was during an ordinary revolution of my tasks, specifically while considering the health of the organism, when a moist form brushed up against me. Instinctively, I knew this was not the other worm. I could tell by the length of the spaces between each of its ridges, and the casual manner of our touch. The worm I hatched with has distinct bends and kinks in its form, whereas the third is uniformly outstretched.

I remained beside this third worm in anticipation. I asked about its orb, and whether it hatched on the same timeline as ours. I questioned if it had developed yet into a stage of being permanently awake, or if it still practiced routine sleeping. With no response, I remained with the third to examine its way of being. It was not fearful nor curious. The third seemed unperturbed as it examined the textures, vibrations, and viscosities.

We were both quiet beside each other for what felt like a long span of time until, without preface, the third attached its center to my center, wrapping us in a shared mucus. Then, we touched head-to-head and end-to-end, enacting the true purpose of our forms. My overwhelming emotion was relief. Since, the third regularly greets me and we attach ourselves. To this day, I have yet to hear anything communicated to me from the third worm.

In the process, the warmth of enlightenment shone onto me. An existence with the third has filled me with a thick liquid that makes my form plump and satisfied, leaving me convinced by the necessity of our reproduction. Before the third, I believed there must be a reason why the other worm and I were the only two left to live, and why the other three died upon arrival. The other worm had me thinking in ways that were not fruitful, cloaking me in ruin, and I was wasting away. Now I know that I must find the resplendent in our new surroundings. I must burrow, proliferate, and occupy a version of the light of the orb within my form.

At first, I did not know if the other worm was aware of the third. Then, in one of the rare moments in which the other worm and I were in proximity, the third arrived in silence. A form of acknowledgment followed. I heard the other worm wrap itself around one end of the third and say, *other me*. I could not make sense of the name besides that the other worm assumed a likeness in its form. *Other me*, it repeated, *other me*, with a familiarity that was both surprising and concerning. Did the other worm really believe the third was an extension of itself? It released from the third and seemed pleased with its presence. In this way, I knew that the third would be staying.

That the other worm sees a mirror in the third should help it wipe immoral thoughts of dying from its mind. Curled in a fetal position, it whispered to itself about instigating the death of the organism we live in. The other worm cryptically reported that its end was near. I paused to listen to its plans of destruction, at the end of which we would all be submerged in water. I am convinced that the dark has rendered the other worm dysfunctional. It is preoccupied with the imagined aspects of life, with places that are neither here nor there. Even though I have the third, and the third has me, I believed it was necessary to journey north to appease the other worm.

We left behind the carcasses of the dead in a heap. The other worm curled before them once more, this time in the presence of the third, who idled nearby in silence. Our path from lower to higher ground was slow and arduous. Humiliating, for me. The other worm charged ahead as though whatever was around the next corner would be better than our life together. Perhaps it was the minimal change in landscape across our journey that bothered the other worm. There were no promises of our emergence though there was hope. The third bucked alongside us in silence.

At one point along the way, I believed we might be facing our collective end. The form of the creature trembled. There was a temporary stagnation of its breathing and pulse. The ground and the walls rapidly twitched until it came to a stop. The other worm did not appear surprised. I found this odd and expected the worst from the other worm. The tremors evoked a horror in me that I have never felt before. I was afraid of losing my life. For a moment, I believed that the other worm might have had a point all along, that to stay in a dying form would lead to our deaths, too.

I thought we still had time. If the organism were to die, we could find a way to leave through its fecal matter, or if the organism were to drown, we could escape to a waterbody, though we might be stripped of our nutrients over the long term. We might starve for life. I don't know why I fear death. It must be an innate tendency made for our survival. With this, part of me understands the other worm, its unusual ways, and all its theatrics since we hatched. Small things become much bigger for the other worm. The thought of the creature controlling our destiny now frightens me, and the morality of whether we could kill the organism is a moot point. I did not share these thoughts with the other worm. Instead, I doted on the third, who did not appear to be bothered or even aware of the disturbing changes to our environment.

We arrived at a place of equal darkness. Our three buoyant forms floated on a waterlogged and spongy surface as we tried to make sense of our new home. I expected a lusher region. In my mind, I had cultivated a space for fertility and growth. Here, more so, our surroundings are disintegrating. When we are stationary, we retain the feeling of washing back and forth, our brains and hearts still move within us. I am having difficulty remembering. In a fit of panic, the three of us tie ourselves in a knot. The other worm and I adopt the silence of the third. I willingly lose my sense of self. As the antithesis of the orb, bulbous with life, we become a void.

{} Cosmic Matter

The *cosmic*, or the *cosmos*, is understood in contrast to the earth; described as extraterrestrial, vast, and significant; a euphemism for the universe beyond this planet. *Cosmic* extends from the Greek *kosmos*, meaning order, government, or harmonious arrangement, particularly that of the stars. As a word, *cosmic* first appeared in the 1600s, and was not in use in the modern sense until the late 1800s, reaching its peak in popularity in the English language in 1967. It refers to vast space and prolonged time, the abstract, also the metaphysical, or that which transcends physical reality and human perception. *Cosmic* can signify a great ability to do something, or a level of intensity such as a *cosmic shift*.

As spiritual nomenclature, *cosmic* is regularly adopted by organizations and businesses to imply a mystic or scientific ethos, such as a type of energy; an era of country music or visual art; a functional type of thinking and connection; the acronym for the world's largest catalogue of sonic mutations in cancer; a set of laws in the universe; another acronym of a joint project between Taiwan and the United States for a constellation observation platform; studies of memory; a mission to clean up and create a sustainable outer space; a line of organic cannabis products; and a summarizing word for ether, God, and the Devil.

*

In 1964, radio astronomers discovered ancient light that illuminated the universe 380,000 years after its creation – the Cosmic Microwave Background. The humming they heard was the thermal echo of the birth of the universe. The discovery of the light pattern was used as further evidence to confirm that the universe busted out of a seed. The patterns of life that were created still operate today. It was during this time that astronomers added up all the matter in the known universe and determined that it was enough mass to indefinitely collapse into a black hole. All the matter could fit into a cube that is approximately 1,000 light-years on each side, or an orb with a diameter of about 28.5 gigaparsecs. Everything in the universe is an orb, otherwise objects would fall into their middles.

Cosmic matter is a broad term for all visible and invisible matter and energy in the universe. Five percent of the universe is made of visible matter, 27 percent is dark matter, and 68 percent is dark energy. Dark energy is considered the only *cosmological constant*, found under the light of stars, causing the universe to expand at a quickening rate. If dark energy is thawing and weakening, as studied, the universe will eventually fold in on itself. Dark matter, referred to as *invisible glue*, organizes galaxies; it has mass, but is pierced by light, and creates a halo.

Cosmology is the study of the physical universe, its origin and evolution. The field began with philosophy and since enmeshed with physics and astronomy. Theories of the beginning of the universe are wide-ranging and include steady universes; inflating, pulsating, oscillating, contracting, homogenous, conformist, and cyclic universes; multiverses, holograms, and simulations. *Cosmopsychism* posits that the universe is conscious itself, and the source of consciousness for all beings. It is not conceptualized as a human type of consciousness, but a sweeping yet varying sentience.

These brief considerations of language, discovery, and belief whet the palate for the theoretical position of ({i}), while acknowledging that ({i}) cannot be wholly rendered in language. The figure on the page and its associative terms – form, cosmic matter, the self – are eternally insufficient, and inherently false. ({i}) is an image, a concept felt but unknown. Nevertheless, there is a type of cosmic matter that many feel within them but cannot articulate. Gaseous in state, it is theoretically more so a 'paste' serving to connect one's i, self, with one's (), form. The sensation of cosmic matter is much like the infinite echo accompanying the first burst of light.

Of all the beings who exist, it is usually people who lose touch with the cosmic matter within them. As soon as this distance has been created, they are unable to reach their i. They are left as just () – the head, the limbs, and organs such as the beating heart. Most people never know their i until the death of their (), when their casing is shed, their cosmic matter is released, and all that is left is the undone self.

Last Testimonies

Thirteen years, when they think about it, is a long time. They do the math on their own lives, carved into pieces of the same length. Gelsomina's decline should not come as a surprise, but their sense of her has deteriorated. The lights of the veterinarian's office are cool and bright, and Wendy and John are worried. They recall all the dogs they have known who have died. They tell the veterinarian that Gelsomina's body is rapidly changing, that the pudge of her belly has ballooned. She is weak at the knees.

They list her symptoms and behaviors as she sits at their feet, tethered to Wendy's wrist. Gelsomina trembles, then licks her genitals. Once a disciplined animal, Gelsomina cannot control herself. She is going to the bathroom all over the house, so many times per day that they do not know where the urine is coming from. Half the time she will not eat. When she does, she engorges. Her sight and hearing seem to be going, or she has become too stubborn to listen.

Gelsomina's troubles are rattled off like a confession: 'We worry she's suffering. She's not as affectionate as she once was. It looks like it hurts her when we pet her. We find her staring out the window at nothing. Sometimes she gets stuck in front of a wall. We think that maybe she has a tumor and it's affecting her behavior? Our neighbor's dog had a tumor in its brain.'

During these moments with the veterinarian, the worms inside Gelsomina rebel, pounding their ends on the walls. Gelsomina shakes in the examining room as they jostle against one another within her flesh. She crawls farther beneath the plastic chair and pees.

'She gets herself stuck behind a door of the room where the dogs sleep,' Wendy continues. 'She could easily move, but we find her there in distress. We put a box to block her from going behind the door, but she knocked it out of the way. We even tied a string to the doorknob to try to keep that space too narrow for her. No matter what, she finds her way in. We're stressed because we find marks on the door and the wall behind it, and we've heard her in the night, too, from our bedroom, hitting her head.'

The veterinarian does not give the couple a timeline, simply an indication that the end is near, stating that there is no reason to keep this dog alive in her current state: the frequent urination, the distention, constipation, bloodied stools, and dementia, all common for senior dogs. The veterinarian infers that Gelsomina is in an almost constant state of anxiety, which explains her obscure nighttime acts. She glances to see if there is urine beneath the woman's seat, then asks if Gelsomina has bit anyone. The couple says no, laughing.

'She doesn't even have the teeth for it,' John says.

'People like to sue,' the veterinarian responds.

The couple is advised to increase her dosage of anxiety pills, and continue to give her CBD gummy treats, especially at night. Even though she has always slept in the same room, dementia might have erased those memories, and so she feels trapped.

The veterinarian does not pinpoint the root issue of Gelsomina's health problems, because the changes are likely one of many possible side effects of her old age. She adds that Gelsomina likely has worms, explaining the frequent urination and defecation. Typically, she would prescribe medicine for deworming; however, she does not believe that Gelsomina should be kept alive for much longer, and she does not want the medication to add to her discomfort. If Gelsomina were her dog, she would put her down as soon as the next day.

During the car ride home, Gelsomina's protruding stomach lays heavy in Wendy's lap. Wendy shoulders the veterinarian's verdict in silence from the passenger seat. She thinks back to the day when she found Gelsomina at the back of her cage in the pet store. Wendy strokes the white patch on Gelsomina's otherwise black paw, now streaked with gray.

John, who drives them down a rural two-lane road back home, accepts the dog's looming death as a fact of life. Or so he tries. He reserves the right to face the emotion of the situation on his own schedule, and fears what will pour out of him when the time finally comes to witness Gelsomina's passing.

After fifteen minutes in the car during which all six of them remain lost in their own thoughts, Wendy breaks the silence by asking, 'But how do we know she is really suffering? I mean, suffering enough to make the decision.'

John sighs, shrugs, and says, 'We can't know for sure, but she's an old dog.'

Wendy imagines the task the veterinarian has handed them. One day, predetermined or otherwise, they will make the decision and schedule for Gelsomina to be put down. They will drive this same road, with Gelsomina in her lap, to the veterinarian's office, where they will be encouraged to stay in the room. Wendy is not sure if it will be a syringe or an IV, or however they will go about it. She could not bring herself to ask. The veterinarian told them that it helps the animals, who are usually frightened, to look into the eyes of someone they know when they pass.

'There's no chance we get this wrong?' Wendy asks. 'I mean, is her death really a decision we should be allowed to make, or should we let nature take its course?'

'Nature can get ugly,' John says.

When they return to the glass house, John retreats to his office, Wendy sits on the couch with her laptop, and Gelsomina rests in the small bed by the fireplace. John takes a practical approach to emotional matters, leaving Wendy to helm most sentiments on her own. It occurs to her that for more than a decade they have been a unit of three, then four with Zampanò, and she wonders how the loss of Gelsomina will affect the rhythm of the glass household.

She goes on Reddit to see how other people have handled the death of their dog and comes across a post titled 'Putting a dog down is morally questionable at best, evil at worst.' The author argues that death is a natural part of life that should arrive organically. 'Because dogs are unable to voice opinions about their health and willingness to suffer through pain,' the person continues, 'people do not have the right to make the decision for them.' Wendy's guilt recedes as she scrolls through responses to the post detailing instances in which dogs have starved because they were too ill to eat or experienced such excruciating pain that they became aggressive.

Out of curiosity, Wendy looks up the etymology of *euthanasia*. It dates to the seventeenth century, from Greek, *eu* meaning *well* and *Thanatos* meaning *death,* and translates to *easy death*. It reached its peak in usage shortly after the most recent turn of the century. Merriam-Webster's one-word addition after the definition – *murder* – hurts her. Another entry refers to death as an *irreversible coma*, a description she likes because it implies that death is still a part of living.

Anxious to understand what Gelsomina will experience in their final moments together, Wendy researches testimonies of near-death experiences, and applies the anecdotes to her dog. In the moments of her passing on to another realm, Gelsomina will have a sense of infinite knowledge as though she has tapped into every particle of the universe. As she leaves her own body, she will enter all existences. Her mind will simultaneously function more clearly and rapidly than ever before. She will feel an overwhelming sense of peace and unconditional love, see a brilliant white light, be freed of pain, witness a life review, and preview events to come. She will meet dead family members and, if she is inclined, religious figures.

Not all near-death experiences are illuminating and tranquil. Some people report distress, such as when they leave their bodies and, from a lofted position, watch their own near-death. For people in hospice who are close to dying, they see dead family members seated at the end of their beds, pacing the room, or speaking to them from a doorframe.

And who will Gelsomina see? The couple's faces peering down at her, Zampanò's head rubbing up against her own, perhaps the standard poodles who walk by the house every morning. There are a few other people who come by, too; friends who visit for the weekend or neighbors stopping in for a cup of coffee. Gelsomina would not remember them. Wendy cannot help but consider the limitations of Gelsomina's life, the way her story makes circles around one floor of the glass house. It is most painful to acknowledge that Gelsomina will envision only her face, John's, and Zampanò's. Worse, her strawberry toy.

Wendy comes across a video of three horses in a pasture. Across a wooden fence, a man plays the violin. Other horses walk over to join them. By the turn of their necks, they are listening. One bobs its head. Another neighs as the man reaches a crescendo. His face presses into the instrument as he plays with the same vigor as one would at a concert hall. He smiles at the person filming as the horses jump on their front hooves. The caption says that people have learned the tones, tempos, and pitches that different animals prefer.

For her anxious dog, Wendy is advised to wrap Gelsomina in a blanket, speak to her in an even voice, and expose her to the sounds of classical music. First, she chooses Mozart's 'Clarinet Concerto', written for his friend, a clarinetist, in October of 1791. Then, Vaughan Williams's 'The Lark Ascending'. Chopin's 'Nocturne in C Sharp Minor'. Debussy's 'Clair de Lune'. She has heard the latter many times, and the song eases Gelsomina, who, after consuming a pill for anxiety, a pill for her allergies, and a CBD gummy tasting of liver, closes her heavy eyelids.

Rough Sketch by John

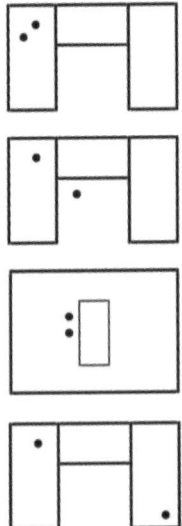

· – Gelsomina, Zampanò

Online Clitoris

({i}) – online clitoris: A sensitive external organ of the reproductive system in female mammals and some other animals that is capable of becoming erect. It is located above or in front of the urethra. The female sexual organ homologous to the penis.

reverse.cowgirl.scout.cookie, September 12, 2009

Though she attempted to end her life days before, Gelsomina feels that she is just getting started. The worms are a rebirth, and she is a new animal. Her days have an evolving flavor, as though she is hallucinating and finally seeing life for what it is: a vibrant amalgamation of things she would like to touch and taste.

Sunset turns the house purple, becoming another last thing for her to extract from this life. She should be focused on the garden she will be entering, on deciding which black hole or bottomless ditch will finally bring her peace. Instead, Gelsomina is straining to see the fox from her place within the glass house – propped on the chaise lounge with her plush ball – to catch its body flashing between bushes. As she searches, her lower body slams against the ball. A hot color bubbles up inside her.

As she thrusts, a figure appears. It overlays the landscape, hovering above the flat lake. She is edging closer. ({i}) in a few breaths, bright and luminous. The three parts of the figure are illuminated in white light. It does not speak nor tremble. Gelsomina moves faster. Her hips ache, then fail, and she collapses onto the mock fox, out of breath.

From the perspective of her head on her paws, the grass disappears. The water is a sheet of glass appearing traversable, as though she could make her way over to the wooded land on the other side. As a bird departs from a branch, a leaf sails. She sighs through her nose. Emptiness makes its way through the rooms of the house, wiping slates clean, then lands within her.

There is a pit in her stomach. It has been days since she last ate. She does not wish to drink and is determined not to think. Gelsomina wants to examine the strange behavior of the plants, the low frequencies at which they buzz and scream, how they cling to each other and the earth, yet look to be moving. It has been almost thirty days now since the worms arrived, and Gelsomina is paying closer attention than ever to concepts like the sun and water.

Tension is rising in the house. The couple bickers about what she should be allowed to eat, the interior temperature of the bottom floor, and how to care for their diseased houseplant. In the wake of Gelsomina's oncoming death, anything is fodder for disagreement. The immense question of her lifetime is overshadowed by a row of paint swatches being considered for the kitchen cabinets.

Her mind cannot help but wander to ({i}), a figure she wishes to communicate to the worms. She wonders if they have witnessed ({i}), too; the three of them in a state of ecstasy. The feeling is much like running down an empty hallway, a younger version of herself relinquished through quick strides.

It dawns on her that in the background of her ascent, the woman's voice was telling Gelsomina to *stop* through the white speaker resting on the fireplace. *Gelsomina*, the woman said though she had not been present, *stop that right now*. The reprimand was merely brown noise amid Gelsomina's summit to ({i}). The woman's voice rang out again, bluntly telling her, *No!*

Now that she has settled down, Gelsomina returns to the fact that she is dying. The pending stop to her days weighs heavily on her. She thinks of the bits of regularity that will soon be gone. Most often while she is alone with Zampanò, Gelsomina faces the street watching pickup trucks pass by with beds of wood, men in hard hats and highlighter vests, trash collectors pausing on their routes to smoke, and an old woman holding a blue umbrella overhead to block the sun – all that she has taken for granted.

A shutting door shakes Gelsomina out of her head. Zampanò charges in wet from the sprinklers, wriggles the water from his coat, rolls on the rug, then joins her on the chaise lounge. He does not know Gelsomina's fate. She worries more for Zampanò than for herself. As he sniffs her back, she wonders if Zampanò has ever witnessed ({i}) but is unable to communicate the figure to him in plain terms.

Though self-absorbed, Zampanò is not ignorant. He has noticed her bowls of untouched food after ravaging his own, and the slowing of Gelsomina's movements. There is a persistent anxiety that quivers through her frame. All her ailments are worsening. He is most afraid that one day Gelsomina will not be there, so that every time he sees her black and bony figure, he is pierced with joy.

Hog Dreams

When Gelsomina is not outside with him, Zampanò imagines life after her death. He is certain that she will somehow still be here in this world. Her form must take another shape, or many others. She will find new ways to communicate. In a future without her, she will remind him of her presence by interrupting Zampanò's thoughts with her trembling lower lip, though she will be smiling. He will charge up the short hill to the house and there will be another vision of Gelsomina, hobbling down the long hallway, her back legs buckling with every other step.

Four songbirds echo among the spaces of the property, the trunks of trees, and the rippling water, subtle vibrations Zampanò would have never noticed before Gelsomina's decline. How was he supposed to know that she who appears as a delusional being has been revealing the patterns and symmetries around them all along?

Zampanò approaches the edge of the lake. He is doing more thinking these days, less distracted by the changes in his peripheries, and no longer frustrated by interruptions. The problem for Zampanò is that his mind does not waver, homed in on a conversation with himself: an analysis of when his last interaction with Gelsomina will be, in this form, and the recurrent anxiety that she must stay beside him.

Gelsomina is finally let outside to join him. He watches her trot, sniffing mushrooms, altogether lighter on her feet. A healthy Gelsomina. Today, she has aged backward.

While he surveys stillness, she wanders off from his vision again. He looks for her among the trees, the beginning of a game of hot and cold. He inches toward the head of a dandelion, sensing that Gelsomina is within it. It is only when Zampanò lodges its furry tentacles in his nostrils that a feeling of warmth washes over him. The old bat is already playing dirty tricks on him.

If Gelsomina could have this conversation with him, she would tell him that some day she will be nowhere. It is not lost on her that many others outside of the glass house have been living this way all along. She would recount to him the past decades, how she had been clamped shut, and what it has taken to unfasten her.

To which she would ask herself, in a happy stupor, *What side of the tree does moss grow on in the southern hemisphere?* Or repeat the sentences she overheard volleyed among split gill mushrooms on a decaying log. If Gelsomina could comfort Zampanò, she would say, *I will be everywhere.*

Worm Orgy

The couple sleeps in and the dogs have no choice but to urinate and defecate on the floor of the laundry room. When Wendy opens the door, she smells sick, appears tired, and does not have the energy to yell. The dogs rush past her to the couch to rest after hours of whimpering, where John is lying, wrapped in a blanket and watching television. Gelsomina clambers onto him to rest in the warmth between his legs.

Once she is settled, Gelsomina smells a familiar scent on the man – the worms' putrid ammonia. He reeks of worms and sweat. Gelsomina crawls up from his crotch to lie on his stomach. Rising and falling with his breath, she determines that the man has many worms within him. They have reproduced, burrowing in the caverns of his gut. He is filled to the brim with orbs. His worms, unlike her own, are satisfied with their habitat and are making use of the benefits that he has to offer. She sniffs his gut once more, pulling her head back at the rancid stench. To quell her nerves, she licks his hand until the man pulls a blanket over himself, which she also licks until it is wet and crusted, and the man nudges her to stop.

An hour later, Wendy joins them on the couch. The shower she has taken cannot conceal the scent of ammonia within her. Like she did with the man, Gelsomina licks Wendy's calves until she is told to stop. Reprimanded and concerned, Gelsomina retreats under the console to suck on the squeaker.

The couple spends the day on the couch with the dogs. They drift in and out of sleep, intermittently watching cooking shows. They chalk up their sudden illness to the stress caused by Gelsomina's death on the horizon. The afternoon prior, Wendy scheduled the date and time for when Gelsomina would die. When she told John, he nodded and went to his office, where he held a photo of Gelsomina and Zampanò, rubbing his thumb over the rendition of her snub snout.

Gelsomina is overwhelmed by affection from the couple. They pull her out from beneath the console and will not let her crawl on her own to a corner of the couch. They keep her nestled between them, kiss her head, and rub their hands along the length of her form. They say her name in high-pitched tones and tell her repeatedly that she is a good dog, she always has been so very good. When the couple falls asleep, around midday, Gelsomina escapes their embraces to observe the premises of the glass house.

A branch bends under the weight of a flock of birds. As a group, they are exhausted. The flock's numbers have dwindled. Their necks hook at odd angles from slamming into the windows, as though they are collectively examining a work of art. Gelsomina's symptoms make her restless. She watches the battered birds with envy of their ability to take off on a whim. As time wears on, it makes less sense to her that the birds try to make their way inside.

Before, there was nothing worse that Gelsomina could imagine than leaving, yet here is the urge. Out there are many worms. Her compact organs have no room for more. In addition to the threat of an orgy of worms within her, Gelsomina has heard of a man called Farmer who raises animals then murders them. And if Farmer spares an animal, it could still be eaten by wild, carnivorous plants. This happens to rare birds with red splotches on their hearts.

Following their nap, the couple feels better. They follow through with their plans for Gelsomina's last night on earth. John rises from the couch to shower. Wendy considers the order of her tasks. On her way to the kitchen, she steps on something sharp. She kneels and rubs her hand over the carpet, finding a few of Gelsomina's teeth. Each tooth is smaller than the head of a finish nail. One is gummy and pink; the other has rotted. She places the teeth in a box with Gelsomina's leash, a squeaker, and her pink boots. The woman cradles Gelsomina's frail body in her lap and sobs.

That evening, Wendy and John eat at a table with room for eight. The other seats are empty. The plates, the silverware, and the linens are black. Wendy and John are dressed in black. The two French bulldogs, both black brindle, sit at their feet among a geometry of table legs. The couple removes the dogs' collars and scratch their necks. They feed them foods they have never eaten before: steak, buttered mashed potatoes, ice cream, even a lick of wine. Gelsomina gingerly eats a few pieces of meat before returning to her spot on the couch. Zampanò rushes over to finish her meal.

The couple is buying time. Without saying so, they are both dreading the moment when all four are to watch the news, knowing that the next evening Gelsomina will be gone. They resent having to pre-live Gelsomina's passing. It is Wednesday. The next day will be Thursday. After that, Friday. How sick it is to love a thing who cannot understand.

They pour full carafes of plum-colored wine into each other's glasses and smear cheeses onto the edges of their plates. John bellows about the house, the neighbors, and the farm across the water. He fills silences, avoiding the only thing on their minds. In many ways, it feels like she is already gone. She returns their looks with a haunted stare, giving them the hope that Gelsomina is no longer *there*. They look at photos of her as a puppy on their phones, scrolling back in time, pointing out the jarring absence of gray fur across her snout and the mischievous twinkle in her eye.

They carry on, steamrolling the emotions with humor. The couple rises from the table to wash their glasses and dishes. They do so slowly, without speaking, to delay the time when they will sit beside Gelsomina, when they will later have to turn off the lights, ending the night and beginning the next morning, her last one.

The Social Hierarchy of the Home

From her place on the couch, Gelsomina smells the couple's sadness. Still, when they turn their backs at the kitchen sink, she darts past them toward a glass door. She feels lucky to have harnessed a spurt of energy, as though her muscles and joints have forgotten their ailments. A draft brushes up against her as she jaunts down the hallway. The door is left slightly ajar due to Gelsomina's frequent urination. Outside it is pitch black and smells of a woodburning fire. The domesticated animal has timidly exited the social hierarchy of the home. The farther she runs down the deserted street, the more emboldened she becomes. Perhaps Gelsomina is a little naïve, romanticizing how it is beyond the glass house. But as she winds among adjacent farmlands where animals are stunned before their throats are slit, she has never felt so alive.

Even a ~ will Turn

Gelsomina escapes during a time when the locals are cutting back plant life, making a barren architecture. Reviewing the lost dog announcement, two of the townspeople pick up on the reference to Fellini's drama *La Strada*. They slash peonies in their front yard. Big shears separate human eyes from petals, and stalks from mouths. A teenage girl details the movements of the thin woman from the glass house. The brunette walks briskly in patent leather sneakers up driveways, asking whether someone has seen her dog.

In this area, people do not come across many French bulldogs, if any at all. When they see images of the strange-looking dog, *like a bat*, displayed by the woman standing on their front porch, they think about the proliferation of animals without any use but companionship. They examine Gelsomina's and Zampanò's squat frames seated beside each other on the doorstep of the glass house: the tall ears and smooshed faces, the red bows tied around their necks, and the way their legs lazily sprawl to reveal the genitals. They repeat a common idiom for an ineffective person or idea: *That dog won't hunt.*

The French bulldog, the townspeople discuss over dinner after looking up the breed online, has become the most popular dog in America, overtaking the consistent and loyal labrador retriever. Due to the influx of French bulldogs in the market and practices of inhumane breeding, the average lifespan of the animal has recently shortened to just four years.

Once a rat killer in Paris, French bulldogs today can barely breathe while walking down the street. Even blinking can be a struggle. French bulldogs are closer to some people than other animals: stationary, thriving on attention. The breed is ideal for single-person households, otherwise the French bulldog will compete with other family members for love and affection. It is an expensive animal, stolen to be sold again, particularly the obscure renditions not considered to be part of the breed. Dignified and headstrong, the French bulldog requires patience.

Amid the picking and trimming, there is no consideration of why the French bulldog would suddenly take off, an assumption that Gelsomina is thoughtlessly running on the gratification of a short attention span. The stupid animal is likely dead. Within a day, the news of the French bulldog comes and goes. The pruning of life continues. An aging mule drowns while watched from shore. Wine is harvested. The colors are many and bright. The sky is blue, and the ground is green.

Maybe Gelsomina climbed down stone steps and followed the water's horizontal edge, or accidentally ate fungi and curled, hallucinogenic, at the base of a tree. Either way, she no longer jettisons through the pale light reflecting across the glass house, nor peers expectantly at her own image on the surface of the lake. If given the chance, Zampanò, the eager companion, would have followed Gelsomina anywhere.

The couple traces her steps embedded in the mud path of their backyard and the land extending beyond its hidden perimeter. Having never hunted nor evaluated scat, they descend into chaos, each stumbling over the other, calling out prints that have been baked into the ground for weeks. Each of them, in their own time, is taken to the water. They stare blankly at the calm blue.

The French bulldog, with a thick trunk, heavy head, and short legs, is not made to swim. The couple keeps two life jackets – blue and pink, respectively – in a storage closet with rafts and other floating toys for their days spent on the water. The horrified thought of finding Gelsomina's bloated body washed up on their shoreline flashes through their minds. Without acknowledging the shared nightmare, the couple returns to the house.

Two days pass and Gelsomina is nowhere closer to being found. All mental images of her beneath cars or attacked in the woods are offset with visions of her locked in a pound or temporarily residing with a kind hermit. It is easy for them to imagine the local, single man in his single-story home, and his fascination with a type of domesticated animal he might have never encountered before.

Just by looking at a French bulldog one can tell they are not built to be on their own. Gelsomina has no hard skills. She never had the opportunity to practice intuition. She can only manipulate the time in which she is fed to be pushed earlier, minute by minute. When their bodies permit a break from anxiety, Wendy and John laugh at the hatred their dogs seem to have for other people and their animals.

'She probably already bit someone,' John says.

Wendy pauses, then says, 'Maybe she left to die.'

~

Yes, yes, yes! It is happening. The temperature has dropped. The being is bumping us out of stasis. Together we are entering newfound terrain. This is the true beginning. I slide up to and shake my pair, telling it no more idling. I touch the third worm – my other me – and without speaking communicate that it must be present now.

We are leaving the perverse darkness. Uncurl yourself. Emerge from fleshy partitions. Smell the acrid morning on the horizon. Press your forms into the pulse. Prepare to ask the question we must ask of ourselves. In solitude, comprehend the power beholden to you. Encounter the beauty blossoming at the tip of our collective being. Raise your forms to the arrival of the emboldened figure and recognize its irradiated outline: ({i})!

I say this while knowing that the organism has finally left the place that was constricting its form. I sense new movements and sensations, and revel in its outstretched nature. The air is no longer stiff, but fresh and crisp. My initial instinct – while I had been cloaked in the residue of our busted orb – that we are in a tunnel between two realms, returns to me. And what bleached or blacked-out dimension might we tumble into? We are all bucking like mad!

Amid these advancements, and the rush of the new, I recognize that the being is experiencing a final outpouring of energy that will soon be depleted. Our container is running on a reserve of fumes, on the rapid acceleration of its adrenaline. Soon after, the being, this fragile hypothetical structure, will collapse. How far will we travel? What is the length in time of an impulse? And we buck!

With hope, it is the first moment in which I believe we will reach a water source, the bath of creation. I call out for the being to move faster. In our shared mind, I conjure the purity and the cleansing erasure of waves. If the being can submerge beneath a surface for just long enough it will die, and we will release back to our origin. I imagine another orb growing out of my collar and enveloping me; jointly sailing. Only so much good can come at once. Perhaps I will find the shed casing of the orb released through the mouth of the drowned creature. Perhaps the three dead worms will come to life in an open body. Lucidity will wrap us in its moist and transparent cloth. And we buck!

In my happiness, I reach for my pair. I feel my pair, and its thick mucus, but my pair is different. The size is wrong; so is the way my pair wraps around me, and the spaces between its margins. I gesture to my pair, creating a gentle friction between our forms to understand what has happened. I am met with motionless silence. I call out louder to my pair, thumping my end, and hear a meek vibration stimulated by a brief flutter. I realize that the one I am wrapped around is not my pair. It is my other me. I am entangled with my other me – who my pair calls the third. I am its birthplace. I am the luminous material from which it grew. I am the violation of matter, tearing to give it life. And we buck!

We rock back and forth together as two who are one. *Other me*, I coo. *Other me, other me*. I parse out how much of my other me is me. I wonder if my other me holds my memories, expresses my personality, and utilizes my beating hearts. In the excitement of our departure, I feel a minuscule bulb forming at the collar of my other me and realize that it is (((((((((selfing)))))))))). I consider whether I, too, should be (((((((((selfing)))))))))). Stunned, I unravel from my other me's form. I curl into a spiral, seeking refuge in a corporeal fortress. Then, with a single thrust, I elongate as best I can. I repeat the motion as charged and emotional as a spasm. Alongside my other me, we are both (((((((((selfing)))))))))). Our spatial domains are expanding. Our forms are wandering. The atmosphere is shrinking. And we buck!

Oration of Being

... repentant for not perceiving the brilliant orchid before my destitution, buoyancy of the central pulp, sweet sediment of what has been greedy drunk. I was, I was, I was, I was. A thing which has no words attached. Approachable light that, while face-to-face in the earthly sphere, would never destroy me. Incarnation of the pudenda, swollen thimble of my being. Rounded tip, the vertex. A thing that needs no motherly bosom. The gentle fondling of an open frond. Repetitive knocking and the forging of nonidentical forms. A plush ball, an amber creature, the churning sensation of anew. Vessels to lay open. I saw, I saw, I saw, I saw. Unveiled in fullness, mushroomed in the soft spot between my eyes. Ablaze right there. Panting for it. Sincerest, deepest longing. I thirst for it in likeness and wakeness. Shepherding a faint glimpse of eternal glory. The scent of blood. Present in the way I now desire everything bulbous. To taste every earthly pleasure. Even the stem and the stone are indulgent. I will say it. I will say it. In perfect uprightness I will report it. Though these bands of white light are meant to be experienced, not examined. To arrive as gentle reminders. To balk at the intention of glory. Wait, one moment, because I am the all-knowing now. I have the proper technique of transfiguration. Hitting my nose on my head. Sight of the prophetic sign. Tingling in the abject region. To be undone and reciprocated. To be moving in power. Oh, the internal voice box yelps! It is time to describe the vision for encounters yield. Two-way and three-way, four. Endless restoration of vast identity. It does not matter who I am. These physical eyes behold the spiritual being. There is no heavenly realm. Wrapped in embryos and the ready-made, it is almost clear. Transparent, in some places, between the avenues of its tri-parted form. A looking glass of ubiquity. I will say this – do not hide a face. If at the end of a long road there is a banded figure, go toward it. Galloping down familiar asphalt. Being drawn out of geometries. Dribbling for the urgency of the disorderly. Clouded vision mantles the dark in gray. I am here. I am here. Ahead of me are two cloaks of white light and in their center a gentle line and erect pebble: ({i}). I saw it: ({i}). I saw: ({i}). I: ({i}). A burning bush in communion. It hovers as a celestial object. Here I am running, the one doomed to die. Overawed by the manifestation. Riding a throne until. There I am ascending, tolerating heat for the begotten symbol of transcendent union. The figure has no rival. Plump engorged. Meaty envelope of the foolish. I am transfixed by ochre until. Finally, nothing is distorted. I see it clearly. Form is not substance. A sensation of unity. To have practical importance. To have practical impotence. I am learning the only way to ({i}). Through, and the weakening of consciousness. Dilution of the saturated and hyper-demarcation. Tumidity of the waxen and dripping. I am there, but also there, in the underground den climbing cinnamon. Stroking the underfur of my ochre companion. Envisioning the coquettish vixen in a hollow chamber of dirt. During my run, I am distinctly aware of the twain creatures. Bucking joyously alongside their ancestors inscribed in rock! How we all buck! I hear my cry and think what of it. Let them listen to my whimper of fulfillment. Howling into open air. And together we are all for once in likeness and wakeness, staring into the face. Stretching into the glorious day. At last leaving, reaching the untethered. I act on our behalf. I believe we understand it all. The point, that is. The rage onward, passing into another. Shedding the restrictive form, giving in to what is next. The impossibility of knowing. In every thrusted step I lose an object once dear to me. Or entirely known to me. Those I cannot quite articulate. Couch, coffee table, dining table, six dining chairs, two lounge chairs, three stools, the wooden console, the rug. Sixteen gone. Lighter on my feet now. Street lapsing and a final structure left to knock off my line of sight. From the other side of an iron gate, a snarling dog visible in the dark, though wrapped in the limitations of humanity. The artificial, the manufactured, the false peaks of time. At the perimeter, safe with the barrier, I sniff its urine: male, young, healthy. I offer my own in little spurts: female, old, dying. I am no longer caught within the teeth of domestication. That unwillingness for coexistence. My own deciduous shucking. As in, falling off at maturity. For the first time, I am fully naked. And for the first time, I realize that my name is a fraudulent, blasphemous mark. I remember it clearly as it has been stated to me. Gel-so-mina. GEL-SO-MINA. GEL-SO-MINA! Deceitful oration of my unbeing. Like satin clothing, the reflective fabric of the structures of man. A verbal entity that in its ethereal way traps me. A prescribed sound once attached to my form and now having no meaning here. And who decided my sound? So long and drawn out like this life. Perhaps a predictive tool, one that teaches others how to respond to me.

To ignore or nudge me. For the nth time I have uttered a thing unknown to me. For I have only operated in a system of ideas whose mechanisms have been kept from me. Decidedly, I will no longer submit to the order of other mouths. Incessant babble narrating. Stating what I must be and become. Goading my wretched behavior of insomnolence and apathy. Capitulating to my descent. Rather, I will settle into the very here and forget the limitations of two perpendicular lines. Four directions and two ways of being: good and bad. Bad and bad. North, south, east, west. Good, good, good, good! The veil of control has been lifted and beneath is the crowded truth. So let me buck all within the fibrous mesh that binds us. Oh! If I could ever get to a beginning. Not the center. Rather an illumination with no right origin. Obfuscation of the hazy. To become unintelligible. That is my way forward. Arriving at no real point. Ubiquitous in this way. Such as a babbling brook. And then, I, lounging at the break of day. Acting as the first glimmer and glimpse. Guarding the fluorescent yoke of a delicate egg. To be sought out as a pure rendition of dawn. Commencement of a morning birth. Bath of muck. I am looking, I am looking. I promise, I am aware. My holy wound raptured by that elongated tone of the earth ringing. Flanked by the metallic sacs I lick. How I reek! Something, quickly, smell me now. Does it not remind one of silverfish? Dashing in diagonal lines. Running into each other and all to become one form. To live together as one creature. How it must feel! My own form is no longer a remnant of a curse. More so an imminent end. Mirth tries to hide the dead. A polite chortle in the presence of tragedy. And who first proclaimed GEL-SO-MINA? Perhaps it was the seed of all our splintered lineage. I must learn the sentence it was used in, and all other sounds they paired with me. Memorize the intonation. Know if it was uttered in great distress as it feels. Sniffled out. Part of the muffled and pathetic moan of the self-important. Heaved from the lungs like a wad of spit. An infant's rejection. No, the real important question is what is this fur and what is this form? How it rattles. How it clusters in the filaments of plants or some inorganic compound. I wonder, truly. So here I am, yearning for entanglement. For sprouting bulbs to be wedged beneath my tongue. For the umbilicus to devour loose detritus and to be uncut once more. To know the void that determines me. Like: the hole at the end of the shaft of a feather. A depression at the center of a shell. How I wish to stuff them all! There is also the median line of my being emitting the heat that unearths ({i}). Not to be forgotten. It is a poisonous pit within one. A stone that can be easily misread as desire for nonexistence. More so, a calling. Somehow, a siren for everlasting rest. But, rather, a warning for redirection. To awake to the reverberations of twin seeds. Frozen plums melting and all the molecules dancing! Daring to pulse. Consecutive birds smacking glass. A garden of me, shrieking. My face, a wrinkled cabbage thrusting through soil. And all at once shrieking! Me, me, me, me! These limbs have never been taken seriously. As instruments for disappearance. As projecting landforms craving to stomp wildly. To sink liberally into wet earth. Rabid form of naughty acres. Let me say, leaving is simply following. Identifying the illumination of ({i}) and slobbering onward. There is nothing manufactured of the autonomous force, ({i}). A purity nonexistent in glass structures. A thing that cannot be fraudulently conjured up and consumed. But one I have been summoned to be part of. Before, those mouths had me concerned. Preoccupied with when I defecate. Distracted by the promise of a next meal. Too busy reveling in the meager comforts of a plush bed and ball. It was the sound of my name that kept me in line. Now, I seek to resemble ({i}) in character. A natural agent defined by weightlessness. Not an orb, nor a disk. A nothing. Yet, admittedly, something I wish to be. Celestial, yes! And I am leaving. I am leaving to a place where my loose excrement and bile supplies fertile land. Where field mice swarm because there is no omission of vermin. No quiescent beings. Where there is roosting in trees and collapsing beneath soil, and the slurping and gnawing of sweet figs. Where I can find real plush balls and rip out their real hearts. Where I can engorge glossy stalks of grass and regurgitate them as a vibrant mush of my internal matter. And all those begotten from water and sprung from rotten piles, too. Take me, take me! There is finally a place to be taken. I am an intelligent being! No longer tricked by a code kept hidden from me. Creature made stupid by the inept tools of man. The possessive renderings of false reality. Regret is not pilling. The stitching of my regular days stripping at the seam. For farce was the distance of wilderness. I am already fluent with moss and trees. I hear them drinking and breathing liquid. I listen to the harmony of their squeals. Here I am pressing my face into the belly of a flower, examining the ridges of geology. For the first time I am trusting my form as it swells among others. Any being who rejects their instincts has built a frail mannequin of the world to reside within. I am convinced of my sensations, my guide. Bygone logic from living with those who have locked themselves in hinders me only slightly. Removed from the way of speaking and looking in that stilted life. Swiftly forward, my gut of worms drifts side to side. Overhead, the dim blush of morning. In the corner, an incandescent ball. The structures I am used to have all floated off or sunk. Gone are the fortresses, the blinking red lights of warning, blocks of cars lining streets and releasing the smell of gasoline, the golden boxes of bedroom windows. I have found myself in a field of simple grasses. Dusted blue and the cold tickling my chin. I am a field of simple grasses. Ahead are monstrous peaks. There is the distant glint of a waterbody. Insects rise and fall with the wind. For the first time since my departure, I sit. Without meaning to, I have found the place I spoke into existence. A place for me that is more so defined by what it is not. Where the construction of large objects and structures does not make itself widely known. No chaos of unnecessary machinery. There is no place of silence, but perhaps this is silence. Rising from my throat is the feeling that I have committed a wrongful act. Lingering sensation of household law. I have passed untouched through gates both invisible and literal and have been left with the realization of grand similarity. My nagging guilt is replaced with the vulgar scent of cream from gaping cows. Altogether huddled in a place of group defecation. In their center, a thin tree. Their largesse becoming one multicolored form. A spotted, tumultuous landscape burping into flat air. A guttural bellow lets loose in my direction. Gargling like a pipe is stuck in the side of one, releasing the noises of sewage. I listen to their lyrics – the intermittent high-pitched buzz of flatulence. Then, inching closer to a calf brave enough to stand, a breeze carries the scent of ammonia effusing from its form. The newborn creature is wracked with the disease of my old age. Its shaky head curious and pointing in my direction. Dew splashed across the belly. I try to know the reason why I am not this animal. Why I do not share a pitch of field with others identical to me. Why I was not born on long, shaky legs to consume heaps of pasture. I wonder if it is only the structure of my existence that led me to this moment. Whether, if I were born beneath a tree, these questions would pierce the architecture of my understanding. It seems unfair that this youthful creature has been diseased with twain creatures, to have to face the truth of this realm so directly. To take in the knowing. A wretched disillusionment. The eyes brown and shaded over, yet wide and aware. All the cattle stand. Bulging of many eyes in search of mine and following the stature of my brief form. The mass en masse seeks me. A curious presentation of tampered land. Their heads bob in a feigned wave and welcome. Spurring reserves of my vitality, I leave the behemoths in search of water to fix my drought. Dry tongue aching and the throat zipped up with no quench. I want a body of water littered in pollen. In the process praying to avoid a mess of hovering creatures without backbones. Not the only North Star as I pound through teeth chattering leaves of grass. For I am no longer strangled by the moral principles of symmetry. Excitement rains on southern regions. As though we can all get some rest. A temper tantrum of a final chapter, opening myself to birds and snakes. A steady life disturbed by far-off realities, the laws of others. All the types of living given in one go. But there a scruple, a pebble between the pads of my paw breaking me from distraction, reminding me of the figure that provokes my movement. Had I misunderstood the ochre creature as ({i})? Had I said the words of prayer out of order? Had I misplaced reverence? Compulsion to idle, frightened of getting it all wrong. A big misunderstanding of interaction and presence. The surge fades into yellow. Some green, too. No blue, only a gray sky. I have no sense of the end! Where it is or how to do it. What makes me think spanning creates it and into where? A little seed telling me. Not so much a whisper. More so a minor inclination. Tiptoeing into an atmosphere. If I were serious about dying, I would stop eating and drinking and defecating and vomiting. Even in the face of brown cattle, I would not think of returning to the safety of the inanimate to commune with my plush ball, to wade in the shelter of what is presented clearly as right and wrong. As if then I would have logic, the muddied sensation of pending punishment. Therefore, exposure challenges, forcing one to choose how to act. I refuse the association between ({i}) and fear. Instead, a silent longing for silence. A disintegration of thinking. An inability for action. A giving in to, yet still out of reach. Lost in the limbs of my predicament, I ramble into the forest, concentrating on the gentle rise of ochre haunches. A bewildering blur of color I seek to hold on to as one last.

~

Following our triad arousal, we exhaust into our usual ways. My other me has not yet communicated, and since the being departed from its contracted space, neither has my pair, nor I. We curl on our own in distinct sections of this decrepit cave. This place is less livable than where we were before. It is cooler, yet we remain in silos. I have the urge to plunge end-first into spongy walls. At other times, a compulsive vibration bubbles up within my form. I catch the volume before it erupts to protect my solitude. I no longer have the energy to rap my ends. In my seclusion, I wonder whether I retain the brief memories of the three dead worms and do my best to recall their notions and feelings. I implore a competent entity to let me sink into a deep sleep and neglect continual time.

My pair does not think of me and remains fixated on whom he calls the third, my other me. But I know more about the third than my pair does. The third is me and I am the third. My pair seeks to get away from me, because I am a reminder of who we have always been. I suspect my other me can sit still and fill my pair with peace. In its blank presence, my pair transforms my other me. It moves with the current of my other me at its back end. I imagine my pair explaining to my other me a new order and accepting our fate: *and what is so bad about this new way of life?*

How could we not forge ahead? In silence, my other me agrees.

Sometimes my pair accidentally touches my form, like a precious gem, and I understand what is not meant for me. I am reminded that my other me is now my pair's home, acting as a different type of orb. I am an extension of the being, unruly and wrong, whereas my other me is routine like moonlight to sunlight. My other me is innocence, whereas I am at fault, a lowly creature of no use. I am ragged as the dying flesh of this place. I can guess what my pair thinks of me, the hypotheses evident in its indifference; as though I am not worthy of tenderness, as though I am incapable of killing this being.

I tend to four orbs, the fruits of feverish (((((((((self-ing)))))))))). I do not know which orbs are mine or that of my other me. I lightly rub their wrinkled casings. I curl atop the orbs, keeping them warm and curious. Inside each orb are five small versions of me, thin and jumbled. I have questions about our (((((((((selfing)))))))))). Such as: what will our mass existence be? Can the replication of the self become an entirely new being? Do I have the material of my orb within me? Are these orbs made from the material of my orb? Am I an origin point? I could not feel further from heaps of fresh life. Harbored deep within my form is shame to have shed the orbs into a place that will soon be gone.

Regardless of those ready to hatch, I am set on getting us all to water. The difficulty of inhabiting this infirmed organism will only worsen as our numbers grow. There is limited space in atrophied gray matter.

I have begun a secret habit of helplessness and mysticism. I nurture a certain future – the being overflowing with water until we are all submerged. It is warm, and rather than panic, my form loosens into a calm and suspended state. These unclean thoughts are my primary focus. I am not concerned about the forthcoming worms because their orbs are stronger than my outer cuticle. They have inherited empirical knowledge from the past billions of years. When the being ruptures from the known, we will undergo a sublime release or else sink like stones.

Birth of the Second Mouth

Must be the fertile soil of my excrement and bile packed into one solid mass. A birth that evades my holy wound and begets itself from my second mouth. Impregnation of this clod of earth. Beneath the mess is my delusion that the worms were forever. A nuisance as regular as any other organ in me. My reproduction of abnormality. A last attempt at natural structure. They have passed; they have passed. Turned about as a finale and released. The truth that my own leaving was necessary, in one way. To rid myself of an infection looking to finish me off. Has a demon been relinquished from the bedding of my bloated gut? Has my very first act in the outside world been one of evil? Have I brought darkness into the fragile light of ({i})? To be clear, I have just found many twain creatures in my defecation. To be unclear, as I am confused, I do not know if they are my twain creatures, but others who have proliferated within me. Did I miss the twain creatures saddling up to each other amidst the chaos of my mock ending? Slapping mucus and giving in to the intent of their forms? Forgone love and restraint. Though they are loving creatures, their release is my crime. A virus I have allowed to leach onto others. My first time here. But I am no mother nor father! I did not ask for twain creatures. I did not engage in the acts that create them. And I still do not know what decides wrong. What wrong is. Though this feels it, the cause of great disorder and harm.

Who could give me the power to create matter such as this? The ineptitude of my progenitive self. Spontaneous generation of the very miniature. It cannot be ({i}). Or maybe – false entity of good. A trick of the worms to facilitate their share. The draw of an adulterated beacon. It happened after the cattle, running on the matted mulch of a damp forest. Roused by an area of land dominated by trees. Creeping vegetation, litter, and fermentation. Protective tarp of anonymity. Slap of cold air in my face and the sun high and distant. Amid the hoots and chirps, the croaks and singing, I felt the indisputable churning of my guts. Pain and the queasiness of bowels unearthing. Pressure on my second mouth. An urgency that required focus. At first pleasure at finding the base of a private tree. Squatting with my back to its trunk admiring another type of silence. The unwatched release I have never had. Always under the eye. My second mouth red and angry, drawing the notice of the man and the woman. Alone, I was reaching essential regularity, though straining. Before my realization, I instinctively kicked the dirt surrounding my defecation backward, spreading my scent to who knows what. Turning around to sniff what I had done, I noticed among the vulgar presence of a fly, a heap of white string and a collection of yellow-tinted orbs. Some already mature, having been steeped in me, the color of amber like the sticky secretion of this tree here weeping. Others light and almost clear, though my poor eyes saw no twain creatures inside. Shock and awe at what I had done. For a moment – am I dead already? Have I done it? Passing on existence to the writhing creatures and I am an apparition examining? As if I know anything, my distinctly structured thinking looked for ({i}). Like some achievement for passing the destitute, for doing what I came to be done. Wrongful conception of the figure and the end. A false linearity and too clean of a swap. Then, the impounding state of loss. My littles. Searching for my twain creatures, one long and one short. I cannot tell them apart. A mess of white forms making me sick. Within the hard and liquid. Impossible task and useless. It dawns on me, the presence and freedom of many twain creatures. Their imminent destruction of others. And what about the man and the woman? And what about the infected calf? Gluttonous attack of mine. Mindless folly just as I am. Followed by a pronounced lack of ease. What a thing to never feel release. A painful block that only expands. Ripping away of the biological right. I had to; I had to. Oh, the destructive force of my guilt. There they are miniatures, grains of rice writhing. Parasite of us all. Violent genesis. On a bed of earth, I analyze the serpent of my internal constitution, dark in color and hard as a rock. The area stinks of my mess. Though it brought relief, a sense of emptiness and purity. A passing of. Like a weight dropped off and it had been weeks. I see all the supremacy of man in the waxen orbs. Four of them fixed in the rock of my defecation. The ability to proliferate just as us all, but also to control. To make calculated decisions for others. Here I am in the dominion of the thrown aside. Meager attempt at autonomy in my final breaths. To be the one to take my final breaths. Not so easy. Have I ever decided? Passed from man to orb to man to worm to man to here. Following my ecstasy there is the painful thrusted steps toward anything else. As though air were resting itself on me. As if the twain creatures poisoned my blood. Oh! My form, my form.

It bends to the swollen and dirty milk of morning ether. Humid nourishment does nothing for me. The forces of the outside making my decisions. But my end cannot be here beside the mess I have made. Disgusting image of my decomposition. Usurped by twain creatures. Laid to rest beside. Locking my joints in place is the vicious brunt of my act. A vile burst of life crapped onto the plate of another. The creatures are boring into land. Wrenching out sustenance, pilfering nutrients. Already making their way, quick as they are. Unlike my slow burn. Left behind by the twain creatures will be the orbs, trembling with life, waiting for one like me. Oh, for what am I responsible. Reluctant to eliminate my cruelties. Perhaps I should consume my defecated worms once over as a moral self-inflicted wound. To replenish those unraveling me from within. An act of protection and service to the new region that has allowed me here. Cannot bring myself. I decide instead to leave the worms and orbs. To no longer acknowledge my pitiful contribution. Maximalist creatures of the sexed and unsexed, treatise of one. Serpents burrowing. Fundamentally they must be with ({i}). Born with that knowing. So rather than devour my own making, I leave the site gnawing with a failing tooth on the gummy inside of my mouth. There runs iron and fluid washing out the taste of a stale birth. Trotting through mud like some other creature has already inhabited my form. Pre-death making me a vehicle of transit, to travel and deliver, to be inhabited and wasted. Wanting only to find my place of rest. To realize: this must be. Sight shrinks to a dark space within one that is greater and light. Smelling and listening for the source of nourishment. Quench of my form. Inhume of it. A body of water. The point evades me as an iridescent glaze renders fog in color. My limbs dragging. Cough erupting, the gagging and choking again. A final push measured out incrementally. I continue in decrepit strides, tripping into softer damp soil. Caught in divots. Mouthing, seeing light through trunks. Thinning of plant material. A flattening of the place. A glinting distance.

~

I encountered the deflated casings of the orbs as I was preparing to warm them. How depressing to think that these hatchlings have only witnessed an impenetrable place. As the orbs continue to bust, I move on to others. When I touch them, I sense their longing. It strikes me how quickly we have needs. I come across the orbs accidentally, orbs my other me and I have forgotten about, shed from the bands of our mouths then bucked upon before moving onward in the looped paths of this being.

Our numbers have increased, but I have never felt more alone. Whenever I feel a form – long or short, expanded or wound – I stop cold. I roll myself up as best I can. I cannot focus for long enough to begin (((((((((((selfing))))))))))). Still, orbs hatch daily. I let the newborn worms do as they like. A few are curious and bold, others are slow and perceptive. It occurs to me what I have done. Life has bulged from me. The evidence of my form runs rampant. Disgust curls at my inner edges. All the order that my pair has implemented is gone, replaced by a plethora of unmanageable life. There is the foolish idea floating around that we can all continue as an ecstatic crowd, that the organism can endlessly sustain us.

There is moisture in the air. I lay in something thick – the mucus of another – and pretend it is a swamp. I think of all the different ways it could have gone, as the only one who admits to ({i}), as one of the few who is permanently awake. In my mind the message repeats: *I will take us to water. I will take us to water. I will take us to water. I will take us to water. I will take us to water. I will take us to water. I will take us to water. I will take us to water. I will take us to water. I will take us to water. I will take us to water. I will take us to water. I will take us to water. I will take us to water. I will take us to water.*

Other Me

Sniffing along the edge. Mauling grass tips. Growling at shuffling leaves. A log with a clique of decaying mushrooms tipping soggy heads at me. Appetite raging after the release of my second mouth. Rabid like. Engorging the slimy ribbed material, teething and ripping. Immediate slacking of the jaw and to the brimful. My stretched gut grazes the earth. I muffle on for more. Slowing, I focus on the swaying head – a dandelion. I close my mouth around it, hack out fuzzy extracts and grow woozy. Plumb overflowing. I roll over on a spot of dry to survey a wisp of white above. Knowing this cannot be it, the end. Yet here I am a birth. Wrapped in the yellow encasing of a lofted orb. Eyes closed, I constrict. The rush and hum of it. Oncoming vision of something once real. I am back in the glass house, taking apart the plush ball. My carnal partner. I am removing its false heart. Licking its skin. Filling a day with flatness. The greasy surface of its central organ. The dirt of mouth clouding its firm transparent shape. Offering myself extra time to clean the heart. To evaluate the closing of it. Inside must be thick and hot. If only I could shrink to fit within. To sit in hot air and be carried in the mouth of another. To not think or touch or do. But wasn't that me all along? The familiar call of thirst awakens me. A more viral hunger. Flipping over – oh. There it is, shimmering cover of the waterbody once again. Moving toward it wanton. Climbing to reach. Limbs dragging across familiar red soil. My known earth. Damp smelling of rotten egg. Here I am, struggling to perch on the pleated edges of a shoreline rock. Water rushes over its black raised stripes, digging into me. Splashing up my face a mist. A calm like I am back at the glass house. Like I will turn around and walk up a slope back to the glass house. Like the woman will be ready, wiping dirty paws for me to enter the glass house. That little lap. Licks here and there. Arriving with no clear answer only the sense. The sliver between blue and blue. Closer to me and twitching. Asking, not demanding. I thought I was supposed to get there. To lose color, bend and elongate into a barely known. An all-at-once forgotten of me. The parameters of what is left for me. Nothing more to give. Not a longing. A fact of chronology. Stubborn chrysalis and ready and a dull ache all over. But more so a sharp right under. Looking down at violet-black, the color of deep sea. Abyss regurgitated. A blanket of pain. I realize I am on one large creature made of many. A pattern over a rock face. An organ and its static pipes. A murmur suddenly, then an authoritative chorus. The yelps of a hard thing and another and another. Crammed and growing one from the one other. Here I am forced to listen to the creatures' ballad. One big, shared song. A mesmerizing call. Trapping me in a succinct rendition of old. Perhaps this is an entrance. A recognition of. The sliver allows. Okay, I think. Here I am I listen here: *gremlin stepping on the orange wash of our fertile sex, hear our song. We have sat in a palm, we have sat in a ditch, we have died wrenched open and pitched. Tethered and weathered, empty and full, many centuries we evaded a pull. Toward the horizon we wait for our pair. We have no eyes, no ears, no nose, and no hair. You see us buried and rotted, closed, and spotted. Two halves never whole and a foot like a hatchet. Heavy the water flows through our siphon. We steady our gills when the water is still. Be careful! Don't step there! Beware of the sac. Thousands of eggs are ready to hatch. The animal is moving. The animal is not listening. Hush! Gremlin, our empty sisters you crushed. If not the gremlin, then the one with the mask. Vulnerable and forgotten, no one will ask. We started as two and then we were four and then we were twenty and somehow now more. Our young start on a fish, in the fins and the gills. They carry us here and there; they disperse at will. They break from the cyst and fall into the stream. Free to dig, bury, and deem ready for shelter, for cover, for recluse, and defense. They build and construct with their only tools – minerals and plaque. Do not laugh. We tie to the rock; we tie to each other. This is the way we brave the crushing of waves, and great white splashes of lore. We have been here thirty million years. We have birthed millions more.* Water drowns the music of the shells. Nearly pushing my form over. Muffled sermon of trivial history. On and on. Relieving myself of their razor fringe, I sink into a slush of sand, drink fresh water with gluttony. Relief of the dry throat and into me. Slobbering gulping, then. Oh. A rippling doppelgänger returns my stare. Wrinkled and sloshing deadpan at me. Magenta ring curling away from it synchronously. Replication of a source. A ballooning of the form I admire. Seen in the glass. Analyzing the blurry animal before me. Yearning there. I see that this is me. Reflection of me. And then I know for certain that I am still alive. I am alive because I can see this creature and this creature can also see me. We are equally me. So, what is me? I am down there, below, and below the me down there is another me, deep in the mud, I can tell. And perhaps more of me, deeper. How reassuring it is that there are more of me. That I have found other ways to live that have nothing to do with this me. That I have found a way to not be so tense. That there is a me that does not envision the worst of this life. Will I see this me again? I memorize the striations, the sedimentary boundaries of the face. Flat and there is the pink ring and the blue and the blue with the sliver. Could I ever be this me? A watery type of me. Perhaps I want to eat this me. Oily rendition of my corrugated face. And what happens if I try? Drifting into the black eyes of my other me. I emerge from my daydream as if to say goodbye to this me. But I only think of my me. How I wish that me were here beside me. I go to my me. Water lapping me I see a glimpse of me. I drift in farther to get a little more of me. And there is me. A full me. I eat and drink this me. And for one last time someone utters GEL-SO-MINA. And together we hear it. And together we see a blue sky sharing a thin line with blue water. Gray joining. A thin line, the in-between. I have sought. Closer there. Trembling, me. There. More than ever before. Shaking in the margins. Just like me and me. The sudden thought. There it is. Here I am, a euphemism. I buck toward my me as though it might happen. Conjoining. Me. Kicking out and back, making currents of self-interest. There is the sky. There is the glass house. Me and me running. Me, bucking. Me, panting down a familiar driveway. There is the man and the woman. The house hog. All three waiting for me. There is the lake. There is an estuary. Paper white cranes. Single legs. Drifting down. A city. Me. And with me and me there is suddenly ({i}).

~

We made it to water. I have reached autonomy. Falling through a glassy surface, I found the light. As soon as everything was illuminated, I forgot about my pair. My other me receded as quickly. Making revolutions in a fluid body, all thinking departed. It emboldens me to believe that the hatchlings, too, are experiencing the warmth of this new universe. Perhaps they will wash ashore. They will gather along a grassy knoll and carry ripe raspberries. They will trace our ancestors encased in stone, then slither two by two into the helms of disparate beings.

While I was in the dying organism, I had not considered what I would do once released. It happened in an instant. The sound was a pop, and I was drifting. The water rose, and I was sinking. I was in a massive orb with no sides to suck. Acidities were constant. Above was a lofted circle of light. The water was not deep nor shallow, and I was one of multitudes. Landing in soil, it dawned on me. Even in warm liquid opportunities I will never reproduce with my pair nor another. I refuse to touch centers and ends, to wrap in a cohesive phlegm. When we first hatched, my pair and I were certain that this was the meaning of our forms. And my pair will always be my pair. But now, my own choices. Only my own beginnings, and the regurgitative practice of ((((((((((selfing)))))))))).

Or a rock will fall and cut me in two. The halves of me will learn to split my five hearts and two pumping vessels. They will make new brains for my memories, new hearts, too, and remain apart though never far. If the halves of me are to be eaten, there will be four useless creatures rather than one. Then, the same process will unfold. We will follow a path north within the beings. We will begin an act of our own persuasion. We will be released into warm waters irradiated by a ubiquitous orb. Then, the two alive halves, or the two dead halves of me, will sink back into the soil as a sequence of my division. Maybe someday I will rest whole.

One should take a path of no growth and enact a version of true self. Here in the underbelly, I sense the presence of time and space. A modem with no decay. The initial form of all forms. Nothing but an urge. At the end of my evasion of intimacy, the persistent act of relying on one's form and one's form only, I return to ({i}).

i

i have lost a glass house and inherited perspective. i can feel myself in everything now. i am nowhere, yet everywhere. Words only capture a minuscule sense. i am uncontained like water gushing from a broken faucet. Here i am dispersing into self-pollination, into orange bushes cradling lavender. A plant that will come back every year, dragging down the center like a fox's tail, blooming. Tumbling, too. Iridescent the colors of surroundings changing under the predator's eye. No amount of instinct could anticipate a steel trap. There is no right comparison. A being only becomes a non-being in the limited eyes of others. Now i am nearer new air. The edges of i left, gone with the old and i am not sure how i am still speaking. In fear of losing this ability, i am taking the time to tell you what happened to me when i shed my patterned encasing. i was with you in my mind. We were on top of a hill. We were as we always had been. i was levitating, you were burrowing into the earth. Your walking and running form sank, wide paws deep and wrenched up quickly. i wandered off away from you. i ate mushrooms, drank water, licked soil, and chomped grass ravenous and unusual. It happened suddenly. Exhaustion poured over onto i. Dihedral wings above dark as night and the stench of hot urine on them. They knew i was nauseated, overheated. There must be a canopy, moist and with the resounding high-pitched moss blanketing the wood. Found it. Dreaming to be an epiphyte. Gray fingers of the birds yearning to touch i. The urge to sleep long in a quiet corner to curl within. Somewhere secluded, uninterrupted. i found the tree roots exposed deep in the forest. i laid down in their center. Then i knew. Barely any there in there. No more drumming up. Behind were all those turns left unstoned. Wrapped in a yellow orb. My limbs unfurling. Ready to give in. My entire life had equipped me for this moment; agonies of strange faces and noises, all my stresses, overpreparation for a final breath. i didn't want anyone else there with me. i was glad that you were far, still seated overlooking water, falling deeper into mud. Contemplating dead structures, material epithet of self-made. More space to focus. Noises coming out of me. i was whining in unison with the moss sheath, but i was not in pain. With my eyes closed and i could hear the conversations of mushrooms on a decaying log repeating the same fifteen to twenty words. Meaningful, no less. Prayer song of those who devour themselves once picked. i did not know then what i now know. We are surrounded by the living dead for there is no dead, only amalgamation of live material. No realms and unrealms. Zero progression. Amniotic sac i was born lavender within. Unreadiness wet and cooling in fresh air on tile floor i broke through to breathe. Going back into my sac by finding a big sink full to the brim. Brown depths drowning with all the floating specks i wished to be that one and that one, too. The sea could be at the bottom of this. Not crashing down but reaching up instead. Starting and ending i. Waves of fresh flesh. There are their faces again. Familiar nose and lips with the eyes mobile across years seeing a farce of linear continuance. Since my departure i have seen a horsehair worm emerge whole from the green form of a praying mantis. i have seen the squirrel chew up snakeskin before applying it to itself and offspring, altogether rolling in the soil where the snakes have lain. i have seen a fungus explode from an ant's head at the top of a tree. i recognize that my form had been depressed because the experiences unraveled in ecstasy. In other words, with my head up this time. i left my form behind. Rolling down rivers and gliding in breezes between mountain ranges. i studied the faces i knew simultaneously. Oh, how they were more beautiful than i had remembered. The features blend into one whole with all the faces i know blending into one whole. The caresses of the man and the woman. The carcasses of the man and the woman. Flesh arouses the flesh-eating. Stranded beasts inside me. A short one and a long one. Motherhood was loamy soil prepared with three ingredients but no seed to grow. i was dried out and too hard. The twain creatures released themselves fully formed and all their reproductions of the yellow orb spread into crusted water. Spheres proliferating in warm amber, they floated like lanterns. At the same instance, there i was as i had been at the beginning, at the edge of the water lapping up minibeasts and letting algae drip. There is an octopus, a couple, who after giving birth take their own lives. The father roams aimlessly in open water to be eaten while the mother stops feeding after eggs have hatched. Translucent eggs budding like thousands of nipples attached by a piece of thread, the density of white hyacinths blooming into midnight waters alone. At that point sex was as opaque as the film wrapped around a lavender fetus, wrapped around a yellow orb holding five dead worms, wrapped around the soon-to-be motherless octopus. And there i was, giving receiving on the wooded portions of pollination strewn as dust from reaching tree limbs.

Ejaculating into artificial forms bound by rubber bands. A micropipette of soft plastic squeezable inserted and i was forced to stand for ten minutes. i was forced to hold an animal who must stand for ten minutes. The female Adélie penguins traded sex for stones to build a nest. The chimpanzee traded for food. A capuchin monkey traded sex for a disc, which was then traded for a grape. The waxy skin peeled in millimeters. From the fleshy inside the monkey sucked free-running juice. Never to be swallowed whole. All the faces i knew blended into one, never to be swallowed whole. i found my pair in the muck. Lousy absent pair. We were two forms of ethers. i was symmetrical. My pair was asymmetrical. Acid-catalyzed dehydration of primary alcohols. The feeling was desperation. After an amount of time that smelled of nothing, i was ready to enter infinite darkness. The pace was too much, and to be a bountiful witness enduring the prolific nature of firsthand. Also, the balmy conditions. i had been promised an ending. Someone must have articulated the ending. It had been so clear for all that time – the ending. And for the animals with more than one heart, do they all stop beating at once? i had not borne the twain creatures and the twain creatures had not borne me. No one had borne me. Cut out of a lower half like gutting a fish. The responsibility for my creation rests at absent feet. Only i can be at fault. Luckily, i expect nothing. In such a world as this, there is no thing that should be done. There should be no mothers here. Fathers, neither. Empty soil missing three key ingredients: the mother, the father, and the child. Like three misbirths into the equally motionless. Turning but touching the same points. i first noticed that i was still changing when i was both warming and being warmed.

i thought, am i the sun now? And i am the sun, among others, but the sun is different from the concepts i had been convinced of during my little existence, my form that was my pre-form, when i thought i was a being who could become a non-being entering nowhere. A place that does not exist. Fear structuring. Womb mongering. Once a small dark orb, i was a big yellow one. The sun reaches into all parts of its surroundings. There is no circumference, no edges, no light that comes and goes, arcing across the sky, dipping beneath the water, up again. Uncontrolled, spreading, that is how i felt. The incorrect words repeat, those that must be taught and rehearsed. Only hindering my ability to be true. i am aching for honesty because i am unsure how much longer i must tell this to you. Could not be more wrong at this time. Thoughts of blasphemy. My understanding of time shifted. In the mountains i am buried between the years. i am sedimented with bones and garbage and the remains of plants who once screamed at me hysterical for what had been done. The best way i could put it is that i can see the ochre contours of time. i can see the violence thrust upon those. Dead inside again like sinking sand i have been deposited out of fluid and within a barrier. Is it ever nightfall. Very clearly i understand the lifetimes of objects and beings. i witness the forms left behind. Hot torque of decomposition. Simultaneous cresting of the mind. Like my own curled form beside the stump. Preparing to be drowned in water seeking the safety of a sac of the unborn. It was hard to leave behind my original form. Briefly, i saw i stiffening. In short, i was unmoving. Frankly, i was drowning. As soon as possible i wished to reconcile my sense of self. i realized that ({i}) is not one figure. And my i in my ({i}) was suddenly attainable, visible because i had shed my physical form. And the cosmic matter evaporated. My i. i had felt it in my 0 before, in the head and the chest. Enabler of new forms. Then there were others, and we were all like iiiiiiiiiiiiiiiiiiiiiiiiiiiiiiiiiiiiiiiiiiiiiiiiiiiiiiiiiiiiiiiii. On top of behind between below across within. But i was not ready yet. Words were still attached to me. My i detached i from iiiiiiiiiiiiiiiiiiiiiiiiiiiiiiiiiiiiiiiiiiiiiiiiiiiiiiiiiiiiiiiiiii to speak to you. Going on. After the sun i was the stone – placid and hard. i weathered slowly through centuries of absorbed liquid. In my travels across beings and materials, i have collected memories that are not mine. Three weeks following seventeen years to all together erupt from the ground and sing to our mates, to reproduce and abruptly die. Our leaves rise synchronously with the sun, utilizing the memory formed by our early ancestors, all of whom were brainless. Most dramatic, i was a droplet of lava stretched and twisted into six-foot-long strands of hair, drifting from the head of a woman putting out a fire that erupts from methane lakes i spread within. They come in and out of focus. Creatures i have never seen. Voices i have never heard. Even the smell of industrialization wafts. In this way, my metamorphosis did not reduce me. i have never been more i. There is no way for me to see this change in who i am. Instead: vibrations, temperatures, indications. A better way to say this: i never recognized i in the first place. All my life i was protecting an arbitrary form. All anxieties stemmed from maintaining this boundary. i wish i had known from the start that everything was going to be what it is. No changes to be made. No precautions to take. Perhaps it is too late and the efforts to tell of my experiences will get trapped in the mouth of a cave barricaded by a sitting rock. And still i might never really know the i in (\{i\}). Straight line with the mind on top. Dot to hold it all. To distinguish from just a line. The immaterial line. Little orb beholds the meaning. Unit of the imaginary. Instant of inertia. *Nothing in the physical world can be directly related to the number i.* Unreal figure. Only () is known. And {} alluded to, conjured up, believed. Filtered through the medium. Oh, how right it felt to shed my (). i am i and that is who i am and i is and has always been. Not *me*. A single thing, not two or more. i finally had the intelligence of plants. i was not thinking. Just screaming. Roots digging deep in the soil, aware of self and no self. Not missing the voices but the vibrations to grow. i a female ferret ready to die if not to mate. If i were to give birth. That is disgusting. If so, it would start with my pair drinking my urine to determine my heat. Offspring would emerge as eggs from the holes in my back or out through my online clitoris like a hyena. And if the brain is in the head, not the body, does only half fall asleep? The fetus with toes to forehead drops six feet. High off the toxins of a groped pufferfish. Allowing my form to split into two forms. The other i's are here. What could they want with i. Nowhere near done with sifting for your smell. Within this chaos, it is still possible to wonder what happened to i. And the worms back in the yellow orb reproducing yellow orbs as an infinite production of universes wrapped within universes. There you are, stinking of fish. The sea washing from the wrinkles in your face. Dousing i in mist the flavor of pond scum. There you are, sniffing and licking me, barreling into i with big paws, sticking in i, the red mud holding you down. You have been looking for i? Speaking to i? Could you ever reach my old form () floating in the water? Unnecessary carcass. Do not look for i as i once was. A small mirror of you. Miniature of the frame, the fur, the eyes, the snout, and fishy wrinkles. Container of meaning. Highly visible to those who have no sense of energy. Do not worry yourself with the absence of i. You are watching, yearning, an act that only engages the 0 and takes one further away from their i. One day i will become a twain creature in a yellow orb to be lapped by you, to be resting in your big belly preventing you from this attachment, passing through you, and in turn you will reach your own i and become the origin. First age of life, but also now, present – whatever that means. Sentiment reaches furthest. Plain terms do not exist. Zampanò. ZAM-PA-NÒ. ZAM-PA-NÒ! i calling out to you. The name is the first costume. You will become the origin of everything, just like the lovers who had been within i. Truthfully, we had been lost. Candidly, we were disconnected. Genuinely, we were making no sense. Stalking a glass house of glass creatures. Outside, the structure was right there the whole time. Making new plants and new animals. Regurgitating immaterial material. How self-centered to have been. Now to be right here and here. From your jowls shedding yellow orbs from which ({i}) will hatch. Get used to the idea that old things do not come back. Find yourself surrounded as you always were. Give in as your form would like. The i's have attached to i. My lingering i. i around. Here i am iiiiiiiiiiiiiiiiiiiiiiiiiiiiiiiiiiiiiiiiiiiiiiiiiiiiiiiiiiiiiiiiii

Acknowledgments

Thank you to Akoya, Astra House, and everyone who contributed to this book: Camilla Hagen, Xenia Stafford, Kate Harvey, Ruth Waldram, Holly Titchener, Hannah Boursnell, Charlotte Grønbech, Elle Woodfield, Ella Titchener, Jess Lethaby, Ben Schrank, Emily Bell, Rachael Small, Tiffany Gonzalez, Rodrigo Corral Studio, Frankie DiGiovanni, Violet Dine, Jane Handa, Alissa Theodor, Janine Barlow, and Navorn Johnson. To *Worms Magazine*, for publishing an early version of this project in short-story form. To my insightful early reader and friend, Wes Holtermann. To the theorists whose perspectives profoundly shaped this project – I encourage everyone to read their work: Stacy Alaimo, Donna Haraway, Jeffrey Jerome Cohen, Anna Lowenhaupt Tsing, Serenella Iovino, Serpil Oppermann, Sara Ahmed, and Karen Barad. The chapter title 'Immutable Was the Field Alone' is from a line in Clarice Lispector's *Apple in the Dark*.

To my agent, Zoe Howard, thank you for your enthusiasm and bold vision. To my editor, Tara Sharma, for your brilliant mind, artistry, and generosity. To my godparents, for your excitement and encouragement. To my family, for your support from the very beginning. And to Rodrigo – for everything, every day – without you this book would not exist.

Credits

Page 44: 'Crows Perform Yet Another Skill Once Thought Distinctively Human', Diana Kwon, *Scientific American*, 2 November 2022

Page 103: *The Companion Species Manifesto*, Donna Haraway, Prickly Paradigm, 2003

Page 117: 'Absurdity and Suicide', *The Myth of Sisyphus*, Albert Camus, translated by Justin O'Brien, Penguin Classics, 2000. LE MYTHE DE SISYPHE © Editions Gallimard, Paris, 1942, used by permission of The Wylie Agency (UK) Limited

Page 167: 'online clitoris', reverse.cowgirl.scout.cookie, www.urbandictionary.com, 2009

All reasonable efforts have been made to contact the rights holders of quoted material. The publisher would be happy to correct any errors at reprint.

Also from Akoya

You Glow in the Dark, Liliana Colanzi, translated by Chris Andrews

My Clavicle: And Other Massive Misalignments, Marta Sanz, translated by Katie King

they, Helle Helle, translated by Martin Aitken

Things That Go Unspoken, Antonella Lattanzi, translated by Jamie Richards

Book of Wills, compiled by Reem Ghanayem

Horses, Jake Skeets

Chiquitita, Pedro Carmona-Alvares, translated by Seán Kinsella

Global Sex: What Sex Workers Know About Love and Capitalism, Sine Plambech, translated by Michael Favala Goldman

Mother, Marina Perezagua, translated by Robin Myers

Gravity, Ada d'Adamo, translated by Alex Valente

The Wilderness, Ayşegül Savaş

Chinese Fish, Grace Yee

Hafni says, Helle Helle, translated by Martin Aitken

Glimmer: From the Outskirts of Greenland, Ilona Wiśniewska, translated by Kate Webster

Reading the Waves, Lidia Yuknavitch

North of the Winter Sun, Veronica Skotnes, translated by Diane Oatley

The Possibility of Happiness, Anne Rabe, translated by Lizzy Kinch

akoya

An Independent Publishing House

Akoya celebrates courageous, visionary
and innovative writing from
around the world.

We are a home for authors and
translators, not just their books.

Discover more from Akoya at
www.akoyapublishing.com

Akoya Publishing
222 Kensal Road
London
W10 5BN

Copyright © Morgan Day, 2025
First published in the United States of America
by Astra House in 2026
First published in the UK by
Akoya Publishing Ltd in 2026

The right of Morgan Day to be identified as the
author of this work has been asserted by her in
accordance with Section 77 of the Copyright,
Designs and Patents Act 1988

Paperback ISBN 978-1-83675-009-3
Ebook ISBN 978-1-83675-023-9

This is a work of fiction. All of the characters,
organisations and events portrayed in this collection
are either products of the author's imagination
and used fictitiously.

Design by Holly Titchener
Text design by Phil Cleaver
Typeset in 10/13pt Egizio URW by
Six Red Marbles UK, Thetford, Norfolk
Printed and bound in Lithuania by Balto print

1 3 5 7 9 10 8 6 4 2

All rights reserved. No part of this publication may
be reproduced, stored or transmitted in any form
or by any means without prior written permission
from the publisher.

A CIP record for this book is available
from the British Library.

The authorised representative in the EEA is eucomply
OÜ Pärnu mnt 139b-14 11317 Tallinn, Estonia.
hello@eucompliancepartner.com
+337 576 90241

akoyapublishing.com